FLYING TURNS

NANCY ELVIRA

Copyright © 2019
ISBN 978-0-578-51226-6

Cover Design by Julie D. Womack

Manufactured in the United States of America

Flying Turns Publishing
Cleveland, Ohio

For my family,
who is still waiting patiently for me to find myself.

Flying Turns

Chapter 1

IN THE DISTANCE thunder sounded, muffled and menacing. Dark clouds churned against the sky – the storm was almost on them.

The ocean parted with a long continuous shush as the *Compass Rose*, the great steamer she was, clocked in well ahead of the Atlantic storm.

The crew paid little attention to the slant of the deck and the ominous creak of the unknown that was upon them.

Eyeing the heavy rain clouds approaching, still getting his sea legs, the doorway saved Will from falling as he gripped it with his right hand. He asked, "The sky looks terribly threatening. Will we be safe?"

"We can outrun the rest of the gale, with any luck," Hale said checking the brass ship's clock with his pocket watch, just to be sure. "Only a ship this strong and well-made would stand a chance," he said, staring at the sinister clouds gathering in the sky.

Lightning zigzagged across the Atlantic, followed by a deafening clap of thunder. "We have to get - - - !" The thunder drowned out his words but there was no question what he was saying.

The crew worked tirelessly to protect the ship from what they were about to be faced with.

On the darkened deck, just after daybreak, Captain Hale clutched the lifeline with both hands as he made his way to the bridge. The ship gave a sudden lurch, sending him hurtling across the wooden boards.

"The wind is shifting - coming in from the Bahamas." Hale continued staring out at the storm. He pushed against the panic and ordered his men to stuff themselves into the main cabin. The surf was raging. He shut the door and windows to muffle it.

Something hit hard against the door. The windows shattered. Dim slivers of daylight came in around the banging doorframe as the wind chipped away at it. He latched the door for a moment and gave orders.

"If the wind gets worse, or water comes in, man the lifeboats. I will remain with her!" Hale flung open the hatch and turned to his crew. His voice shouted against the waves of sea spray and air, pelting his face. "Don't latch the doors!"

Never-ending waves continued to loom above the *Compass Rose* in the darkness. The deck heaved up and down. Her bow pierced a wave, and seawater gushed over the forward section of the deck. Will braced his feet, turned his back, and gasped as icy water sloshed over him. Rain stung his face and arms.

The *Compass Rose* hurled and thrashed, turning in circles as if looking for an escape from the hurricane. Broken boards flew across the surface and shredded metal spun, swirling in the air overhead.

The wind ripped the hatch off the deck; it flipped and tumbled in the air. By then, the water was over Captain Hale's knees and the waves were cresting over the bow, sweeping and claiming anything in their way. The rain continued in, seizing and scratching across everything in sight.

Blinded by a curtain of driving rain, Hale called from the rear through a megaphone, shouting through the wind, directing the lifeboats be put over the side and partially lowered. Even if they were able to escape in the lifeboats, the odds weren't in their favor. But remaining aboard would give them absolutely no chance for survival at all.

The storm continued to pound the *Compass Rose*, waves coming aboard, smashing in windows and doors. They huddled below, listening to the wood and metal crack; the *Compass Rose* was splintering into a thousand pieces.

The heavens released a howling fury. The storm raged on, creating several moments of false hopes that the fury of the storm might be over, only to be swept away by the wrath of the hurricane as quickly as hope had appeared on the scene.

The storm had ripped off one of the lifeboats and all of the lockers on the deck. A ladder nearly claimed Will, as it flew past him. The *Compass Rose* groaned, listing hard to port. Echoes of anguish were deadened by the sound of screeching metal.

"*Abandon ship …*" The words strangled in Hale's throat. A sudden gust of wind tore his words to shreds. Then a deafening, rolling, thunderous roar saturated the atmosphere around them.

Suddenly something changed. The wind shifted and transformed into little wisps of air. There was an eerie calmness in the sky. The rain ceased. A thin golden halo appeared around the edges of the indigo purple cloud overhead. The sun was emerging.

One by one, the men onboard the *Compass Rose* gathered on the deck, gazing into the incandescent sky. As relief spread across their weary faces, the jubilation in their voices was unmistakable.

The rose-gold of the sun peeking out around the cloud, seemed to burnish the deck's surface, giving its stacks, masts and everything around them an uncanny radiance.

The sky looked like it had been freshly washed, the air releasing a sweet fragrance as they moved about the deck. They were suddenly very aware of the sun on their faces and the warm breeze touching their skin.

Through Will's blurred vision, he noticed that the deck remained tilted at a strange angle. He marveled at the crew of the *Compass Rose* as they began cleaning the deck of the debris. Emptying buckets of water over the side into the ocean, he found it incredible that they were still afloat.

First Mate, Paul Morgan, appeared from around the side of the cabin and approached Captain Hale. "I think you need to see this. I just saw the damage to the hull." He motioned for Hale to join him. Will followed.

Hale's expression was grim. "How bad is it?"

Morgan gestured as he turned and led him and two other crewmen across the slanting quarterdeck and down below. Hale's head throbbed as he bent over to survey the destruction.

Leaking compartments would have been an understatement, to say the least.

It wasn't possible. Five cavernous holes in the hull, under the sea level – clear through all of the walls - openings they could see right through, to the water – in five separate places. But no water was coming in – not a single drop. He wiped the sweat from his brow. Nobody spoke.

Hale held his hand, the one with the missing finger, in front of one of the gaping holes – the biggest one. Then as he began trembling uncontrollably, Will reached past him and put his own hand completely through the cavity.

"*Ho-ly cow,*" Will breathed as he quickly drew his hand back. It was dripping with water – seawater. He looked at the ragged openings again and did a double take.

Captain Hale could find no words. There was no explanation for it. Was it too late? Were they dead?

By all rights, the *Compass Rose* should have been on her way to the bottom of the Atlantic Ocean. But she was still afloat; her entire crew safely aboard. Hale willed himself to stop trembling like a leaf in the wind.

When they found their way back to the deck, they noticed something. They were no longer slanting. Hale made a sound of exasperation. A loud one.

Was this some kind of message from heaven?

Or from hell?

Chapter 2

WHEN HE WAS a young boy, storms were a source of excitement for Will because of the prizes the current brought ashore. His brother, John, had taught him that for every treasure they uncovered, somewhere, out to sea, a ship had most likely been broken by the wind and water.

Although the settlements along the water's edge continued to claim a tragic annual toll in ships, one man's misfortune was another man's happy windfall. There were buildings standing along the shore built mainly from timbers generated by the wrecks and later made cozy by successive disasters that yielded shingles, hardware, heaters, petroleum and coal.

It was a mixed blessing.

Will spent several sleepless nights, expecting to wake up from his nightmare at any moment and fighting the urge to scream. And when the sun came up, he wasn't sure if he was grateful or not.

After six days of gloomy, gray weather, the sun had broken through shortly after dawn, and the weather deck was bathed in its bright, radiant light. Will greeted Captain Hale on his way to the wheelhouse.

"Today the ocean seems so much more forgiving. It's a bit warmer … calmer. The colors are green and blue, instead of black and gray."

Hale nodded in agreement.

Then Will added, "It's so unpredictable out here, Hale. I am afraid I will never understand."

"After every storm comes the calm, Stockton. But we must learn to sail through the storms so we will never take the calm for granted."

The *Compass Rose*, meanwhile, plugged along as best she could, meeting horrific weather but making the best of it. Unfavorable winds drove her far from any course and monumental seas invited themselves aboard her rudely with great frequency. The days, cold, gray and unruly, dragged on.

Chapter 3

"ARE WE THERE YET?" Yeager mumbled as he passed the wheelhouse.

But where? How much time had evaporated? Their compasses didn't work, no radio reception and the sun played tricks on them – one minute it was in the east and the next it was in the west. They hadn't seen land in days ... surely somebody was searching for them.

And, with its coal-fired steam engine, how was it that the coal supply never depleted? On the contrary, it varied from time to time – the bunkers were half-empty and a moment later they were full.

A creeping, vagueness hung over the *Compass Rose*.

On more than one occasion during the course of the following days, Will questioned Hale. What direction were they going? How long would it be before they reached land? Why hadn't they found themselves at the bottom of the Atlantic Ocean?

Where the hell were they?

And each time, he was met with the same response. "I am the captain on this voyage. You will just have to trust me."

"Trust you to do what?"

"To make good decisions. To do the right thing."

When Will woke the following morning, the briny tang of the sea was the first thing his senses registered when he opened his eyes. For a split second, he forgot why he was there and what had happened. Then it all came back to him.

So much had happened to them; surely, their luck would soon change. But he couldn't help wondering if bad news had no limit.

Will was beginning to doubt his brother's selection of Thomas Hale as the captain for this trip. A captain is supposed to see his ship and hands through a safe and smooth voyage from beginning to end. This had been anything but a smooth voyage. Prohibition or not, Hale seemed to be a heavy drinker and Will knew from experience, that alcohol can severely impair the thought process.

Will expressed his doubts to the second mate and a deckhand regarding Captain Hale. But he was met with nothing but absolute respect and admiration for Hale.

He rolled his eyes. "Yes, but I don't believe I have ever seen the man sober. How is that good for the *Compass Rose*?"

"True, this is his first time as captain of the *Compass Rose*, but he has brought many vessels through rough seas safely, and he has never lost a man on his crew, Stockton."

His eyes settled, but whatever he was going to say was interrupted by the galley door swinging open as Yeager came toward them with an iron skillet.

"I may be up in years, but I'll have you know …" he held the skillet up in the air. " … I have been on dozens of voyages – all over this world! I am more than an old fool! The only captain greater than Thomas Hale is Captain John Stockton!"

The salty old sailor spent five minutes singing Captain Hale's praises, while Will listened with surprise.

Will thought about the look of resolute confidence on Yeager's face when he spoke of Thomas Hale, of the loyalty and admiration he held for him. He looked back at the first mate, Morgan, as Yeager returned to the galley, with a look of puzzlement.

"But he believes in him. He's a good judge of character." Morgan said.

How was it possible to make a good decision when there wasn't one to be found?

Will held his finger up before he walked away. "Good people have been fooled before, you know."

Chapter 4

SIX DAYS TURNED into seven, and then eight, and there was still no sign of land. They had just finished supper and darkness had cast its net over the sky again. They were surrounded by near total obscurity.

Captain Hale had always disliked the dark. It was a childhood fear. But not for Will. It represented a challenge to him. After all, the stars needed darkness to be seen.

Hale didn't know whether it was cold or not, because the alcohol had isolated his body and filled it with a man-made warmth. He put one foot in front of the other and put his senses on autopilot.

Chilly air entered his lungs as Will buttoned the top button on his coat. Wild, dark, beautiful and terrifying, yet hypnotic at the same time, he found it hard to tear his eyes away from her. The sea. He was beginning to understand his brother's fascination for the water.

Will's gaze swept across the sky as if he were mapping out a route. "Everything looks a little odd, don't you think, Hale?"

"Moonlight does peculiar things." Hale was also looking toward the night sky.

"Where's the moon?" Will asked him.

"It must be behind the clouds."

But there wasn't a cloud in the sky.

Will found himself dreaming more than usual; he didn't know which was worse - the dreams that haunted him so much that he hated sleep, or the real world so haunted that he hated to wake up.

He woke that night with a jolt, sitting up throwing off the sheet and landing on his feet.

It was nothing but another lousy thunderstorm that had rubbed his imagination into nightmare. The lightning illuminated the room for an instant, another flash so bright he could read the dates of the certificate hanging on the wall.

Outside, a mighty whirlwind bore down upon them, intensifying with every second. Waves slammed the hull again and again, and he knew there was no way they would ever outrun the deluge. The storm was sitting right on top of them.

In that split second after waking, he felt the relief of knowing it was just a dream, and then the next moment, he knew the real nightmare wouldn't go away. It was still there.

HE STOOD ON the stern, staring into the ebony water that seemed more like ink as it reflected the moon above.

"How did we make it through the kind of storm that sent so many ships to the bottom of the sea?"

"She's a good vessel." Hale put his hand on Will's shoulder.

He looked back at him. "I am finding that harder and harder to believe, Thomas." He turned back and faced the water. "I suppose you are right. After all, our lives were spared."

"I don't think we are alive, Will."

The expression on Captain Hale's face gave Will cold chills. To combat them, his blood began to boil. He was enraged.

"We're dead? How is that possible?"

Hale looked at him testily, not wanting his decision challenged. "Do you have a better idea?"

He didn't. Will backed him up against the rail and twisted the front of his shirt in his fists. "Hale, if you don't tell me what's going on, I swear you will find yourself on the other side of this rail!" Then he paused, and then suddenly released his shirt. "But if you're already dead, what would happen?"

Then, before he had the chance to stop him, he watched Hale hastily jump into the water, with barely a splash. Will clawed at the rail, waiting for him to surface before he began breathing again. He leaned over the rail. "Hale - Are you mad? You were down there a long time!"

Captain Hale treaded water. "I've already tried - I cannot drown … at least not for the time being."

He may not have been able to drown, but he wasn't immune to exhaustion. Hale finally climbed back aboard the *Compass Rose*, and met Will, eye-to-eye.

"Stockton, I believe that the *Compass Rose* is the only reason we were spared a horrible death. There's something about her - always has been."

Will flapped his arms around in frustration. "It's as if my life has become some sort of game where all of the rules were changed right in the middle of it."

Hale shivered in the cold. "I think we are going to have to get used to this."

Will spun around and stared into the heavens. "This is a joke! Someone is trying to convince us that we are crazy!"

Thomas put out a gloved hand and caught a stray snowflake, then smiled at him. "Perhaps. We have more questions than explanations, don't we?"

"Like, why do we still feel things - like the cold? Hunger?" Will buttoned up his jacket to his chin and shuddered.

FOR THE NEXT few nights, sleep was out of the question. Will was afraid if he closed his eyes, he would surely die. He laughed out loud at the irony of his own thoughts.

It was becoming a habit.

Chapter 5

AND SO, AFTER the endurance of two more storms, the eleventh day came. It was colder, the wind had swung around to the north and the steel gray had been replaced by blue skies.

Will had determined that they were already into the gradually descent from autumn into winter. The days were a little less brilliant and nights were a little less starry. He missed the crisp air and turning leaves, haystacks in the fields, fresh apple cider, and memories of Cleveland.

Will woke up to bright sunlight streaming in through the windows and sparkling on the ice-encased rails. He paused and took a long, steadying breath.

Sunrise. It was the one thing they could always count on. Whether they wanted it to happen or not. Every day started out exactly like the one before.

They also found it difficult to remember what day of the week it was. Was it today or was it tomorrow? Or was it yesterday? Time came adrift. The hands of Will's watch either turned too fast or too slow. Not broken, just inconsistent.

Sometimes it was like a great void, an eternal nullness. There was a dead look in his eyes that Will sometimes saw in the mirror.

It seemed that every time they caught a glimpse of hope - hope that they were only moments away from returning to their lives, they were met with crushing disappointment.

Just after breakfast, they spotted an upbound freighter plowing through a storm across the sea, a proud sight with her lights ablaze on the water, full steam toward them.

The crew of the *Compass Rose* shouted and waved frantically to attract its attention, but that soon changed as they flew into a panic with the realization that the freighter was traveling far too fast and too close to them. Frozen in fear, they watched the vessel approach - it came so close that the hands on the *Compass Rose* could see the faces of the crew. The bow of the ship towered above the stern of the *Compass Rose*, bouncing up and down, making its way toward them.

Terror set in, but the freighter didn't slow down. They braced themselves for the impact. But the vessel sailed right through them and it kept going.

There was only one explanation.

The *Compass Rose* was absent - invisible – *as invisible as the devil sitting in the front pew at Sunday service.*

A deafening hush fell over the deck.

Morgan was the first to speak. "Maybe we're a ghost ship" he said, feeling chilled.

Will stared back at him, in silence.

"You don't believe in such things? Ghost ships?" Hale asked, heading back to his office.

"Hardly." Will replied, following behind him.

"You know, Stockton - they can be tricky. Just because you don't believe in them doesn't mean they're not there." He slid the door open and stepped inside.

"Oh, I believe you *think* you know what you are saying," Will chuckled.

Hale reached under his bed and brought out a bottle. As he uncorked it and poured himself a glass, he looked out at Will and said, "Tell me something - is it that you don't believe or that you don't *want* to believe?"

When Will didn't answer him, he finished his thought. "Believe what you want …" He raised the glass to his lips again and returned it to the table in front of him. "… but the seas have many ghosts passing through them. And we are haunted by those ships and those who vanished with them."

Will nodded. "Exactly!" He leaned into the door. "So you see," he said, "the *Compass Rose* couldn't be a ghost ship. We all made it - we're still alive!"

Chapter 6

IT WAS WEDNESDAY. Or was it Friday? One day it was summer and the next day, they found themselves caught up in a frigid blizzard.

Seagulls swooped around the masts while the crew swabbed down the decks and polished the brass.

William wiped the sweat from his brow and sat down, watching as Hale stooped beneath the table in his office, producing a few heavy crystal tumblers and a full bottle of Irish whiskey.

He was surprised that, in light of all the *Compass Rose* and her crew had been through, that bottle hadn't been drained long ago. "How have you been able to restrain from polishing that off, Hale?"

A smile slipped across Captain Hale's lips. "It does tend to knock the edge off things for a while." He patiently poured the golden amber liquid in the two glasses and handed one to Will. Will raised the glass to his lips and Thomas Hale pounded his own down in a mere two gulps.

He turned and faced Will, backing him into a corner, with a crazed look of fire in his eyes. The stench of alcohol burned Will's eyes as Hale breathed in his face.

"I will ask you again. Do you believe in the supernatural?"

Will stared back into his hollow eyes, in soundless question.

The captain elaborated. "Ghosts." He took a long swig from the bottle and handed it to Will. "Our culture does not encourage belief in the paranormal. People who admit to such experiences are often ridiculed and have learned to keep their mouths shut."

Twenty minutes and half a bottle of whiskey later, Hale watched the fright fade from William's eyes as he sipped his drink and stared out the porthole, over the dark water.

"But here's what I do know - I believe I ..." Hale cleared his throat and continued. "... *we* didn't survive that day that first hurricane hit us."

Will sat down hard on the galley stool, the bottle still in his hand, and stared back at him with doubt.

"But somehow, life goes on. We wake up each day and there's a sun, just like always."

Will raised an eyebrow. "Now that you mention it, I do feel pain and I bruise; but no matter what happened the day before, I wake up and the wounds; the pain ... they're gone."

Then Hale snatched the bottle from Will's grip, ran out onto the deck and leaned over the rail, quickly dumping the remainder of its contents over the side, emptying it completely. He held it up to the light and said, "See this?"

A look passed between them. Will answered him. "The bottle? What about it?"

"Why, I'll show you why we haven't run out of this - this devil's brew."

Will's eyes rounded as Hale suddenly threw his empty glass against the cabin wall, shattering it to smithereens. "It's bottomless, I tell you."

Will stared back at him in disbelief. "Bottomless?"

"He nodded. "The bottle replenishes itself."

"You've completely lost your mind." He paused and stood for a moment, in silence.

Will suddenly pointed to the bottle. It was still empty. "See? You really thought I believed you, didn't you?" He chuckled. "You've been pulling my leg, Thomas."

"It's rationed."

"What do you mean *rationed?*"

"It's as if we are only allowed, allotted, a measured amount each day." He leaned in and met Will, eye-to-eye. "It will be full in the morning.

WILL SPAT SALTWATER from his mouth. He opened his swollen, hungover eyes a crack and, through bleary but steadily improving vision, saw the bottle sitting on the floor, next to the ship's wheel. The fire of morning sunlight danced across the surface, reflecting off the bottle.

He straightened to get the crick out of his neck and he spotted the bottle from across the deck. It appeared empty. He scrambled across the floor, stumbling over Captain Hale, and snatched the bottle into his hands. With his touch, the bottle began populating with liquid.

He held it up to the light. It had whiskey in it. Not just more than there was last night. The bottle was full.

The panic in Will's voice was unmistakable. He picked up the glass Hale had shattered the night before. It was intact ... with whiskey in it. Will shook his head. "But how? Why?"

Thomas opened his eyes, struggling to become vertical and looked over at Stockton.

"I don't know!" He flung his hand in the air. After a moment, Hale took a deep breath and answered more calmly.

"But I am sure we will soon find out."

Chapter 7

HE WAS STUDYING the sky through binoculars, as gulls flew and called out, just overhead. Thin, diluted sunshine was struggling with heavy cloud cover. A dramatic ray of sunshine speared through the clouds, then was swallowed up as quickly as it had appeared.

"Hale, you have been out here for quite some time, "Will said, tossing his cigarette butt over the side. He blinked into the horizon, but it was too murky to distinguish the sky from the water.

Overhead, cawing seabirds flew gracefully with rowing wingbeats over the water, swooping down to pick fish from or just below the surface.

Will asked him, "What are you looking for?"

"Variations in warmth … rogue waves. The water temperature can be as variable as the light – ice cold in the deep, shadowed places, and warm from the sunlight in others."

A troubled frown lined Hale's forehead. "A good sailor knows everything is always shifting. The wind never lets the water stay still." Thomas turned to Will and lowered his binoculars. "I have reason to think that we will soon be on another adventure."

Will faced Hale as two of the inquisitive birds landed beside them on the railing. Hale nodded in their direction. "Terns."

"Excuse me?" Will was puzzled.

"Terns." Captain Hale continued. "I have noticed these particular birds in the sky ..." the light in his eyes intensified, "... but only moments before one of these unpredictable tempests begins to form."

He pointed to the north, where a thick haze had rolled in across the horizon. "They are vocal and social birds that make their presence well known. They are preparing for something."

"Will blinked. "You're kidding, right?"

Captain Hale shook his head and continued to study the sky.

"Hale, have you been drinking again? They're just birds." Will gestured with his hands and shook his head. He lit another cigarette.

"And you expect me to believe that these ..." Will walked toward the resting birds, causing them to scatter into the sky again. "... these *flying terns* are some kind of escort, leading us into the path of danger?"

Hale gave out a hoot, and then he slapped Will on the back. "Stockton -- sometimes I wonder if perhaps you and your brother, John, are not really brothers."

Will looked back at Hale as if he had just slapped him across the face.

"... not *danger*, Will!" And he brought a flask of bourbon out from behind his back. He grinned and took a swig. "... **Adventure, Stockton!**"

"There is not one logical explanation to a word you have said."

"I may not be a scholar, Will Stockton -- but I *do* have something out here that all the college degrees in the world would never give me."

Will's breath got tangled up in his chest as he waited for the rest of what Captain Hale had to say.

A fire ignited in Hale's eyes. *"Experience!"*

"I don't believe this!" Will wrung his hands in frustration.

But Hale grabbed him by the front of his shirt, causing him to nearly faint from the stench of the alcohol. "And you will never, *ever* escape that cycle, Will ..." he continued. "... until you *learn* to ... **believe**."

Will pried Hale's fingers from his shirt and threw him backward, with an angry expression that told he was running out of patience. "You are completely mad, Thomas!"

But Hale backed him against the rail and pointed out north, to the horizon. "...it's called *suspension of disbelief.*"

"Hale," Will reaffirmed after Thomas had stopped speaking. "The whole thing sounds flimsy as hell to me."

There was more of a breeze than usual, and it began to smell of rain. Hale's voice softened. "Let it go, Will! It may be our only way out."

Will's pulse leaped and bounded as he watched the circle of birds overhead.

Hale continued. "The water carries with it many mysteries, Will. Your brother, John, understands that."

Will brought his gaze back to Hale's face. "Yes, he is very wise."

"I've known your brother, Captain John Stockton, for a long time. Back when he operated excursion ferries, in Cleveland, John loved to reveal the secrets of the lake, bringing people up close to nature … to bring to light the majesty of the lake, the mysteries that lie beneath its surface and a reverence for the earth. He believed that if people experienced the wonder of the wild, they would carry that revelation in their hearts and work to protect it."

They continued to walk to the galley. Hale coughed. He gave Will a sideways glance, "You know, John has told me that he thought you could learn a thing or two out here."

The atmosphere had turned stiflingly thick. They felt a powerful surge grab hold of the ship.

"*Shit!!*" Captain Hale disappeared quickly.

Will, his eyes upward, instinctively grabbed hold of the rail, detecting the massive dark shadows gaining on them. He studied the billows that were forming overhead and felt the side-to-side rolling motion of the ship.

He eyed the racing clouds. They seemed to be in a big hurry. Without warning, there was a particularly dramatic sway of the ship. The first heavy drops began to fall. He pressed his thumbs to his eyes.

The rain was coming from the southwest, smacking against the windows on the unprotected side of the ship. The rain dripped in diminishing lines from the overhang, like a beaded curtain, but the deck itself was bone dry. The list was not severe but seemed to be increasing steadily, and for no reason.

A jagged burst of lightning split the clouds over the ship. Several seconds later, Thunder boomed.

The wind picked up. The sea surface peaked into sharp whitecaps that began to break over the stern. Lightning flashed and more thunder followed. A thin sheet of water poured in over the low side.

When Hale's rudder manipulations and more speed on the engine failed to keep the *Compass Rose* headed into the wind and seas, the vessel growing more sluggish with every passing moment, Will concluded that foundering was not only a possibility, it was imminent.

Thunder rumbled in the distance and lightning slashed through the sky. The *Compass Rose* lunged like it had been punched by a giant fist.

Will was hoping that Hale's theory would prove to be a figment of his whiskey-soaked imagination. At any rate, this time, he was resolved not to hide. He dropped behind one of the lifeboats.

He heard a distinct sound. The stillness of silence.

Something suddenly burst into the air. Then, one by one, he heard the beating of wings overhead.

Terns. They were everywhere. Will raised up, in awe of what was transpiring before his eyes.

As he stood, he felt a feather-rush of air, touching his eyelids, his cheeks and his mouth. Something he had never sensed before. He craned his neck to the sky and, in an outright paralyzing moment, he froze in disbelief.

Repositioning themselves in midair, the terns had created a vacuum of sorts - a flurry of wings pulling the *Compass Rose* behind them like a wagon following a child on a summer day.

For an instant, he could see for miles, across the seascape of waves, partially hidden by the white froth that poured from their tops, as if the ship was sailing through the storm clouds themselves rather than the ocean.

The *Compass Rose* twisted and turned, the water struggling to hold them earthbound. Then, in an instant, they went from the pull of the earth's gravity, fighting to keep them, to a feeling of weightlessness. They were flying upwards ... suspended for only a few moments.

And then they took a sharp turn directly into the clouds.

Chapter 8

IT WAS THE part of the evening where dusk dissolved into night. The *Compass Rose*, once again, had survived the storm, battered like a bruised fighter.

Hale was on his third shot of rum. Or was it his fourth? He couldn't remember. He stumbled across the room, sending the glass crashing to the floor. Faces and voices swam in his memory beneath his closed lids. He gazed, with unfocused eyes, at the new, gaping hole in the hull of the *Compass Rose*.

HALE PACED THE upper deck for hours before returning to his cabin. His life had changed dramatically and, while he tried to be strong, he was still shell-shocked.

Had Hell already arrived?

Will walked past the open door and, seeing the vacant expression on his face, he entered the room and sat at the desk. "We wouldn't have been the first ship to be swallowed up and disappear from the face of the earth, never to be seen again."

"Why in God's name were we spared?" Hale asked with a red-hot fire in his eyes.

Will took a cigarette from his pocket and stood.

Hale continued. "But for some reason, we have been spared." Then he smashed the bottle against the wall. "Is that good or is that bad?"

Somewhere, off in the distance, he overheard the faint rustle, out on the water. As it got closer, Hale recognized it as the rustling of another vessel. But not that of a steam freighter. He closed his eyes. And he pictured masts, and sails in the wind.

A schooner. The kind his grandfather had sailed in the nineteenth century.

"But who would be out here in this weather at this time of night?" Will asked.

The mercury appeared to have fallen considerably, but there had been no sign of snow. Not optimal conditions for a cruise, no matter how large the vessel might be.

Captain Hale peered out the porthole, not hearing a word Will had said. He wasn't sure at first what he was seeing, but soon there was little doubt.

Caught in the light of a full moon rising in the east, illuminating the way, were flags. And sails.

Will followed Hale's gaze and saw a small schooner heading in their direction - its wake, a white, churning tail. Then, it stilled. There appeared to be nobody on board.

And it didn't move.

They attempted to shoot a line across to the vessel, but the wind made it utterly impossible. As the lines fell short of their target, the captain tried again the dangerous dance of positioning them nearer to the bow of the schooner. As the Compass Rose maneuvered closer, however, he realized the schooner's bow was surging - both vessels could collide, killing them all. Or something close to it.

The captain decided to edge away, hoping the storm would subside a bit. Even if it did, he wasn't sure they would give it another try or not.

Hale turned to Will. "It wouldn't be prudent to approach them at night. We will all take turns, standing watch, just in case there are pirates on board. For our own safety, we will board the ship at sunrise."

Maybe in the morning, the clipper would be gone. Maybe in the morning, they would be back home, in the port of Cleveland. Maybe in the morning, this would all prove to be a dream.

But not likely.

Chapter 9

OVERNIGHT THE WIND lessened, but a thick, impenetrable fog had set in. It was impossible to see anything more than ten feet away. Their plans were involuntarily placed on hold. When it lifted a day and a half later, the schooner was nowhere in sight.

During the latter part of the two days of fog, they heard the sounds of a foghorn. Captain Hale said it sounded to him like the horn of a ship - there was no mistaking it.

They knew, by the age of the schooner, that it couldn't have carried such an instrument with it. Everyone was excited at the prospect that they had been spotted by another freighter, but frustrated by the lack of visibility.

The foghorn of the *Compass Rose* wailed, as if howling for its life. The crew shouted with all their might. They banged loudly on anything that would make noise, but by noon, the sounds of the foghorn had ceased; and when the fog finally lifted, they saw that there was no freighter. It was as if some protective shield had lifted from their hearts as well, leaving them clear-eyed and able to see the profound darkness of their circumstances.

The crew had just about given up hope when they began to sense something in the air. A light breeze stirred the surface of the water and as small waves broke against the ship, he could smell the sea in the humid air. But also something else that he couldn't quite place.

A sickly breeze teased them as it blew by, bringing with it the scent of the unknown.

Captain Hale fell to his knees and took out his binoculars. "It's the schooner. They fell quickly to his side. "We can't get too close or they might spot us."

"Would that be bad?" Will was puzzled.

The *Compass Rose* was none the worse for wear. Powered from the stern, her bows carving the water into precise, white slices, she drove on toward the vessel at a cautious speed. And then her engine stilled and they sat.

Will and Thomas continued to study the vessel through binoculars. Littered with masts and spars, hulls and sails and splinters of a lifeboat, the sun cast an eerie glow over the debris surrounding the vessel.

After witnessing the wreckage floating on the water's surface, Will asked the captain, "It didn't look like that when we saw it before. What happened?"

"Only storm energy with a hurricane force would be capable of sending a vessel such as this to its demise, Will."

"But the weather has been fine, other than the fog." Will shook his head.

"I find it rather odd that this schooner of such age and condition would be out here, on the Atlantic," Hale remarked.

But Will rolled his eyes and stared out into the body of water. He tossed a biscuit overboard and watched it quickly disappear beneath the surface, without lingering for even a second. "I don't think this is the Atlantic, Captain."

Hale looked upward. Then he dipped a fishing net over the side, into the water. As he brought it back over the railing, the water splashed on his face. Hale licked the droplets that lingered on his upper lip.

Stockton was right. It wasn't saltwater. They were no longer on the ocean. How could that be?

AS THE LIFEBOAT chains were released, a rogue wave tossed a piece of the boat's bow toward Will and he had to dive to avoid it. They came across the disabled vessel, adrift, a schooner – taking on water.

"Watch where you step," Hale instructed as they climbed aboard the abandoned vessel.

Once they boarded the ship, they were subjected to the gruesome sight of an expired sailor, held up by a life preserver, on the deck, as if to be welcoming them aboard. Evidently, he hadn't had the opportunity to try it out.

The deserted feel of the vessel matched the way Will felt inside.

Hale, Will, along with three hands who had accompanied them, used searching poles to prod through the water, looking for bodies of the crew. Or survivors, but the latter was highly improbable

Wood weathered to silvery gray covered the floorboard of/on the deck.

How could this be? The ship had just met its fate only hours before.

And yet he was stepping over splintered rails, pitted with salt and mildew. And age. There was no doubt in Will's mind that the vessel had been like that for quite some time.

A lightning-like crack in the hull reached from one end of the starboard side to the other.

The deck was empty – void of all ornamentals that should have decorated the bow, except for a worn carving on the bow that resembled a serpent. At least it might have been a serpent at one time. The only other thing that remained was a starboard lantern.

Will ran his hand along the casing. "A work of art."

All four of them couldn't shake the feeling that they weren't alone. They continued with caution.

Will felt foolish all of a sudden - like a child afraid of the dark, afraid of ghosts lurking in the shadows.

A flock of terns suddenly filled the air, circling and dipping overhead, chasing away the ghosts.

Hale and Will went below to investigate, with caution. They stepped watchfully down the staircase to the lower deck.

Ice water rushed through Hale's veins at the site. Will's breath caught in his throat, and his heart pounded so hard he could feel the veins in his neck throb. They both wanted nothing more than to turn and run, but they remain rooted to the spot, unable to make themselves move.

Four corpses lay on the floor -- lifeless bodies. The scene before them looked empty of everything but secrets.

Who were they?

Morgan approached him from behind, carrying a lantern. "What do you think happened to the rest of them?"

Will remained silent – but he knew the answer. They were standing on their graves.

He continued pushing and sloshing the clutter aside and waded through the water, searching for clues.

"The cargo looks to be stone." Will said.

Captain Hale nodded. "Limestone."

Algae had marred every surface. He scratched his name on a porthole. "I only hope that death came with merciful swiftness to the crew. They appear to have been trapped, with no chance of getting outside."

"It looks as though they were somehow sealed in their own vessel."

He motioned to the others as he passed them. "These men deserve a proper burial at sea."

After reviewing the destruction of their surroundings, it was determined that the dead bodies would be brought to the *Compass Rose* and prepared for burial at sea.

Later that afternoon, Hale found Will, on the portside deck, staring out into the water. Will acknowledged Hale, but he didn't move. He spoke. "What kind of a God allows this to happen to good men, Hale?"

"Will -- all we can do is to honor a vessel whose captain and crew have met their fate by welcoming their spirits."

"You will join us, won't you, Stockton?"

Will chuckled. "I would probably scare all the good spirits away. I'm such a heathen, you know."

"Oh, I think they must be used to heathens. If we were all perfect angels, they would have nothing to do," he said with a smile and a wink.

A DEEP MELANCHOLY took hold of the ship. Captain Hale removed a folded sheet of paper from the inside pocket of his coat, put on his reading glasses, and proceeded to eulogize the men.

Captain Hale removed his hat and bowed his head. "Ashes to ashes, dust to dust."

The company of the *Compass Rose* bowed their heads and silently joined him in prayer.

42

"We know not of their circumstances, nor do we know how these souls lived their lives - but may the Lord bless and keep them - and give them peace. Amen."

"They called back, "Amen."

The bodies slid, one by one, from the planks and broke the water's surface with five separate sheeted splashes, each lingering for a brief moment before disappearing, sinking like stones beneath the water's surface into the depths of the lake.

The crew of the *Compass Rose* slowly went back to their duties disappearing to their posts.

Once he had recovered from the emotional turbulence generated by the burial, Will went to the rail and gazed over the side, fighting the first wave of nausea since the day they put to sea, in Cleveland. It was a good ten seconds before he breathed again and even then, it wasn't a normal breath.

"The wind and the mist marks the timeless passage of the lost clipper."

Will turned as Hale joined him. "To be buried out here is a great honor, you know, Will." He sighed. "There are many ways to die. Death from exposure and starvation are the worst."

"That's not exactly comforting, Hale."

"It doesn't look if they experienced either of those."

Chapter 10

"EXPLAIN TO ME again why we are returning." Will said to Hale as they lowered themselves back into the lifeboat.

Captain Hale inspected the drain plug, to be sure it was inserted properly, and he motioned for the crew to activate the davits. As they dangled from the Compass Rose, he answered him. "There's always the chance that pirates may stumble upon a deserted ship, such as this one. And who knows what unsavory purpose they would find for it? It could destroy the legacy of any good that this schooner and her crew worked hard to accomplish."

"So what can we do about that?" Will inquired, as he began rowing.

Hale answered him, without any emotion. "We must sink it."

"Deliberately?"

They boarded the ship one last time to inspect it for weapons and other articles that could be used.

It was decided that Will, being the only one possessing the athletic prowess to even consider it, would make the climb up the rope to the top of the mast, where the only remaining flag was still attached, flapping in the breeze, tattered to shreds. The lone survivor. He carefully raised his foot, eyeing his grip on the frayed rope.

He began the climb, deliberately not looking down.

One slip and I am a dead man. He laughed to himself at the irony of that thought. He removed the flag and set it on top of the starboard lantern, which he had removed earlier.

Hale searched the sky. "We may not have to do much destruction. There's another storm looming … out there, waiting for us."

Will glanced upward as Hale finished his thought.

"By my estimation, we have about an hour before the storm is upon us."

They passed a creaking door, still hanging from hinges though the wall around it was gone, swung slowly. Will hadn't noticed it on their first trip aboard the schooner. How could they have missed that?

In the short period of time they had been gone, the bannister had disappeared, fallen into the level below. The stairs hung from the wall, swaying back and forth in the breeze. How had they not noticed that before? It was determined that it wasn't safe – they wouldn't be going to the lower deck again – at least not unless the floor caved in beneath them. Which was entirely possible.

They continued. The door to the captain's quarters had a hole in it the size of a brick. Will pushed it open.

A shadowy horizontal line, about four feet high, stretched across the captain's quarters. Shards of broken glass at their feet shimmered in the light.

The hairs on his arms stood at attention. "Are we in hell?" Closing his eyes, he listened and heard his own voice echo in the wind.

But then he heard something else … another voice, low and guttural, coming from within the ship, like it was trapped within the walls. He swore it was a voice speaking back to him.

"Wait." He listened. It sounded more like... laughter. And it wasn't coming from inside the wall at all. It seemed to be all around them. He swallowed hard. A trick of the wind, he told himself. The gusts were stronger now, whistling around the boat. That had to be what he was hearing. Then the laughter stopped.

Hale spotted movement above them. He looked up. The motion had appeared to be moving around in the dark upper reaches of the captain's office. "I believe that ships have souls and destinies, and hearts."

What or who could be up there? Will's eyes adjusted to the darkness. He saw there were no compartments, none that were large enough for anyone to hide in.

Thunder rumbled in the distance. Darkness was bearing down on them. Hale was right. There was another storm coming. Waves crashed violently against the hull of the ship.

"The answer lies within the log."

"Thomas -- did you hear that?"

It might have been the lake breeze, coming across the waves, whistling in the sails. But Hale believed it belonged to the captain of the doomed vessel.

Will's heart rate spun out of control. *"What was that?"*

"Not *what* it was ..." Hale whispered. He stood frozen, his mouth open. Then he pointed behind Will. The words sounded brittle, hollow.

His face changed and that cocky assurance melted into fear. "But rather *who* it was."

48

Chapter 11

WILL PIVOTED ON his heels and stopped. Thin, colorless loops of mist seemed to penetrate everything. A ripple of fear made its way down his spine.

The voice continued, but more emphatic. *"The log."* There it was again. The words - an odd parting, to be sure, dogged his steps as they made their way to the door.

A swift gale breeze caught the door and slammed it shut just as they reached it. There was no light except for what seeped in through the slit at the bottom of the door. Their eyes had little time to adjust.

"Meet the challenge of the combination. Find your destiny."

Will swallowed, trying to process it all. Were they having a conversation with a ghost? Half blind, Will felt around in the dark for something, anything he could steady himself with. His foot hit something – the sharp pain in his ankle almost brought him down, but he stumbled on.

Hale stopped to examine what Will had stumbled over. "You found the safe, Will."

"A safe?"

"Every ship carries one on board. Why would this one be any different?"

"What do you think could be in it?"

"It varies. Depending on the captain, it could hold money or jewels belonging to passengers. Sometimes it's a holding place for the captain's journal."

"You mean the *log?*"

Captain Hale nodded.

Will examined the locking mechanism. The base of the safe was held shut by a 4-inch iron jaw operated by a big combination lock the voice had warned him about. The lock consisted of four cylinders - each marked with a series of numbers dash-mounted side-by-side, with a lever shaped like a lion's head on the right. All he had to do was enter the combination, pull the lever, and open the safe - and Viola! That was all there was to it.

But of course, they didn't know the combination. Will tried many different ways to guess the combination. He gave up in frustration. "It's no use, Thomas."

But just as he straightened back up and turned away, the door slowly swung open, by itself.

"Well it's open now," Hale said.

Will returned to the safe and stood still for a moment, resting his hand on the top of the door. He leaned in, pulled out a heavy, wooden crate and handed it over to Captain Hale. Hale lost his grip and the box fell to the floor, its top splintering into pieces.

There was money inside – a lot of it. Gold coins; *gobs* of it.

"We will be rich! The world will be at our fingertips!" Thomas shouted.

Will let out a low whistle while Hale dug his hands deep into the container, stirring its contents. Suddenly, Thomas' hands stilled.

But that would do them little good, in their condition.

What good is gold if you can't spend it?

In a frustrated rage of fury, Hale scooped out a handful of coins and he ran out to the portside deck, where he began throwing the coins overboard.

But Will noticed a tiny sliver of color when Hale scooped a new handful of gold from the box. He yanked the box out of Hale's grip.

Hidden underneath the gold, was a smaller case. Will lifted it slowly from the box.

Captain Hale gasped. "The log." He sat in the desk chair and opened the book carefully. Squinting in the dim light from the porthole, he began to process the words on the paper.

From where Will was seated across the desk, he couldn't see the text, but he knew by the look on Thomas' face that it was either very good ... or very bad.

Captain Hale dropped the book to the floor and hastily ran through the door, to the deck for some fresh air.

Will took a different approach. He picked up the book and sat quietly on the desk. In the increased arc of light from the open door, he held the book at an arm's length, in an attempt to see it better, but it didn't seem to help. When he scooted back further onto the desk, he knocked something off the desk onto the floor. He glanced down and grinned.

It was a pair of glasses. They must have belonged to the captain of the ship. It was a longshot, but it was worth a try.

The wire-rimmed glasses slid low, barely staying on his nose, not a perfect fit, but they did make it easier to read the words in the logbook.

Will made a minor adjustment to the glasses. He steadied himself, staring into the open book, with shoulders squared.

The writing was elaborately formed; it looped smoothly over the leaves of paper that had been torn raggedly. His gaze burnt into the journal as he flipped through page after page. It was like cracking open someone's chest, pulling back the bones and flesh, and looking straight into their heart. Everything the captain and his crew had felt or experienced was laid bare.

Will began reading. Then he turned the page. It took a few minutes before he began to understand. He ran his tongue along his bottom lip. He read with his head bent over the log, his right hand pressed to his mouth and his left hand gripping the edges of the desk. His throat tightened as he studied the penned words in front of him.

He read what had happened to the crew on the schooner. The journal told of those before them - some honorable but many others that weren't – those who chose not to heed the warnings. And they never survived to tell their own stories. Stories of deceit and greed.

But many more of dreams and reality, hope and despair, happiness and sadness. They had been ambassadors, of sorts, although Will wasn't sure what for. They were given missions to complete; missions that would balance out and correct "errors" of time and nature. His hand shook as he turned to the next page. The reality was beginning to take hold of him.

Hale leaned in. "Evidently," he said with a quiver in his voice," they were tied to the ship." He gestured to Will, who was engrossed in the log.

"You have such a healthy skepticism for anything that cannot be proven beyond the shadow of a doubt. How could you be possibly interested in anything having to do with ghosts?"

"Skepticism doesn't preclude curiosity, Hale."

His heartbeat quickened when he realized he was traveling towards the back of the journal, his fingertips skimming the edges of each page as they drew him to the captain's final entry.

Before he reached it, Will paused. Undoubtedly, there would be things, which he would rather not learn, but like a passerby being drawn to the site of a crash, he was unable to look away.

Staring at the final entries, he saw that just one side of the double spread page was filled. The adjoining page was missing; it had been ripped out, leaving behind a jagged edge near the spine of the journal. His eyes fixed on the remaining page, which was filled with random thoughts that didn't seem to explain anything. At first.

But, in a flash, the meaning of the words he had read became crystal clear. A lump pressed against his throat and a bead of sweat trickled down his temple. His mouth went dry. The log dropped from his grip.

He snatched up the journal again and located the single sentence that had pulled him up and made his heart crack; the line that made it perfectly clear: By opening the captain's journal and reading it, by default … the torch had been passed - to them. The true secret of the schooner' strongbox had been unlocked.

"Hale, you know I don't believe in ghosts, but …" Will said.

Will suddenly snatched the glasses from his nose and instinctively dropped them into his pocket. He jumped up "I can't explain it, but I feel as though we are not alone on this vessel, Hale."

When he glanced up, he saw that the room was empty.

Chapter 12

AS HAUNTED SHIPS went, it was a fairly noisy one. Creaky, rapid clicking sounds, but that was to be expected on a ship.

More mysterious noises surfaced, but Will did his best to continue reading the journal. He found it fascinating to learn that the ship had been lost in Lake Erie, over one hundred years before the *Compass Rose* had even existed, and they had been merely wandering.

There was an unsettling groan. Far away, a door opened. Will's heart nearly stopped. He held his breath, not daring to make the slightest sound. Footsteps came cautiously from the stairway above. Someone creeping, hoping not to step on a squeaky step.

Throat dry, they hid in the darkness, just behind the desk, flattened to the wall, the duo was scared to death. The footsteps were louder now. Closer.

There was a low, throaty growl. It stopped, but it came again, louder. Will's heart sped up. Hale opened his mouth to speak, but Will raised his hand for silence. Slow footsteps were passing overhead. With each contact, the ceiling vibrated and the lone lantern dangling from above swayed from side to side. He groped around in the dark to see if there was anything handy to use as defense.

Nothing.

He tried the door. It was stuck. There was no way out. The air suddenly felt hot and suffocating.

Hale took a ragged breath in. "Grab whatever weapon you can.," he whispered, bending to grasp a pipe that was laying on the floor.

A gust of wind whistled through the open window of the wheelhouse, as he breathed in the mingling powerful hints of oils and turpentine with lake air for what he hoped would be the last time.

Will looked upward and said, "Well, let's get this over with." And he prepared to disembark.

Hale stared at him. "I think we should leave as soon as possible, Will." He said in a shaky whisper.

He began backing toward the door, the last glimmer of light disappearing completely.

Stumbling, almost falling, they scurried on. A fine mist from behind seemed to be closing up on them. They heard footsteps and heavy breathing, gaining on them. Running through the dark, they dodged, jumping, fighting whatever it was that was chasing them.

He glanced backward. There was nothing back there. Just an empty space.

Did I imagine all of that?

The idea of ghosts coming after him seemed ridiculous, but he kept his eyes forward until he turned the corner. He could feel the sounds echo as his view of the world became rougher, like shreds of paper at a ticker tape parade. He turned. His heart either skipped a beat or took an extra one.

Shapes emerged from the vapor, in the half-light. Then something hit him in the head.

Chapter 13

JUST BEFORE HIS eyes rolled up in his head, Will caught a distorted glimpse of the monster from across the room, ready to pounce at any minute, the ghostly, warped image sending his heartbeat off on a wild tangent.

The mist drifted closer and the room grew colder and Will shut his eyes to black out the sickening vertigo. Something surged up from below, swirling into a solid mass of light color; he turned blindly only to see it rushing toward him again and he fell, hitting the rickety bookcase with a shoulder.

And then he passed out.

As Will regained consciousness, he felt heavy breathing in his face. He had instinctively squeezed his eyes shut, but he opened them one at a time to see Hale, passed out next to him. Then his heart sped up as he searched for their pursuers.

A close blaze of lightning. And there it was again, a pale wraith, a ghost of a creature, illuminated for a split second. This apparition, for lack of a better word, made his heart beat faster.

Through the haze, he caught the shape of his pursuer, staring back at him. As the fog began to dissipate, he locked eyes with not one, but two of his hunters. Gnawing, head-butting, snapping, growling.

And then they pounced on him.

He reached up to protect his face, but his hand was drenched in a wet, slimy coat of spittle. A sudden tilt of the ship sent Will into an uncontrollable roll, away from the doorway.

Slowly his eyes regained their focus and he made out the sight of two small, shadowy figures scampering across the deck, accompanied by a sequence of *woofs*, tilted heads and questioning expressions.

Huddled against a stack of burlap sacks, they were revealed in a brief flair of distant lightning. He could see that they were wholly consumed by fear. If he hadn't known better, he would have sworn they were member of the canine family.

Finally convinced that they were, in fact, dogs, Will stepped closer, squatted and snapped his fingers. More lightning. Ten seconds and the thunder finally reached, sending them skidding across the deck, around the turn. He wasn't sure if they were running from him or from the sound.

Will took off after them, in hot pursuit. They led him on a chase, skittering around corners and up and down steps.

He eventually cornered the pooches. He dropped to his knees and he held out his hand, coaxing them to come closer. "Hey fellas", he whispered, trying to find the right pitch. "You want some dinner? I've got some on the *Compass Rose*. I won't hurt you. I'm here to help."

As long as the puppies didn't move, Will continued talking like a nervous suitor hoping to impress his date.

Will scooted himself down to the deck and he sat. Slowly, the dogs pushed themselves more upright, cocked their heads and listened to his voice, deciding.

Cautiously, toenails clicking across the deck's surface, the puppies approached him. They stopped just shy of an arm's length. "Well hello there," he said, freezing, with his hair plastered to his head.

He stopped and motioned for the others to come close.

"Dogs?" Morgan asked.

Will answered him "Puppies." He bent down and picked one of them up. "I'd say about three months of age."

"Where did they come from? Dogs don't just drop out of the sky."

"… or do they?"

Will pointed to the flag and the starboard light, preparing to return to the *Compass Rose*. "This is all we will take with us … other than the puppies, of course."

"Who do they belong to?"

With an almost impish grin, Will answered him. "I think we just adopted a couple of dogs."

They lifted the puppies, one at a time, into the lifeboat and set off for the *Compass Rose*.

It was official. Miracles were possible.

Chapter 14

THE DARK DAY turned into an even darker night, as if the sea and sky had merged. The air was black. Raging toward them, the muffled roaring of the storm intensified, turning into booms that attacked his eardrums like a battery of gunfire.

Will grabbed the railing near a ladder. A loud crash thundered from behind. Huge waves battered and tossed them. A low rumbling vibration resonated from the ship as it crashed ruthlessly into the crest of the breaking waves.

He was only halfway down the ladder when the wind hit, leaning the ship to her portside, just about on her beam-ends.

A deep popping emanated from the bowels of the *Compass Rose*. The ship groaned and shifted into a deeper slant. Its bones were snapping - breaking from contortion distress. The rounded stern tilted vertically toward the sky.

The wind brought jagged streaks of lightning and rain so violent that Will thought at first it was hail. It was relentless - the boat rose up as the torrential rain that battered them from above and the jagged lightning split the sky. Will could hardly see his hand in front of his face, let alone the length of the boat.

The rain continued until well after dark. But then, just as quickly as it had appeared, there was silence.

Sunrise brought with it a strange sense to Will. A sense of another chance to get it right.

Life anew. What a concept. He felt excitement and then fear. And then many more fears. This was his new normal. The trouble was normal simply felt strange. Unfamiliar. But most beginnings were like that, weren't they?

Captain Hale joined him at the breakfast table in the galley. When he was met with a look of apprehension from Will, he took a bite of his toast and said, "It's the start of another journey, Will - filled with opportunities you might not have ever envisioned."

Will's stomach gave a little flip of panic as he thought about how long he had been navigating the seas on the *Compass Rose*, walled off from the rest of the world. He took a deep breath, squared his shoulders, and he said nothing.

Chapter 15

BOTH PUPPIES SEEMED to bloom under all the attention they were getting from the crew that afternoon."

They settled back, watching the dogs stretched out in the warmth of the woodstove, the open bottle of whiskey between them. The scene was almost as surreal as the rest of the whole ordeal.

As the gentle rocking of the *Compass Rose* lulled him into a temporary state of serene contentment, Will almost forgot what had consumed his every waking moment since the fateful hurricane.

How had this happened?

WILL WAS STILL in the same position four hours later. Late afternoon sunlight streamed in through the porthole. He had a crick in his neck and his muscles were stiff with weariness.

A faint dusting of clouds darkened the horizon, but that was no guarantee. A storm could blow in quickly.

Consciousness was a struggle; moving was more difficult. At times, it felt like he was sleepwalking, just going through the motions of day-to-day existence.

The dogs were friendly enough, poking their curious noses through the doorways, nooks and crannies of their new home. It was clear that the pair had a family bond - littermates certainly. They carried their tails at exactly the same level and they moved as one unit, patrolling the *Compass Rose*, communicating effortlessly as they kept watch.

Will set down the dogs, patted his leg and walked over to the galley door. The little dogs trotted amiably at his side. He stopped at the doorway to the galley, where he met Captain Hale and the first mate.

He leaned down and picked up the first puppy. "This," he said in a voice filled with pride, "is Hubbell." Hubble gave him a polite sniff and then a quick lick with his tongue. After seeing the question on their faces, he went on. "I named him after the astronomer."

Then Will picked up the second puppy and said, "… and this little girl is Clancy." At the sound of her name, Clancy whipped her tail and picked up her ponytail ears.

Hale smiled and asked, "And who is Clancy named after?"

"I just like the name." He set them back down and beamed as they shuffled their front paws. They stared up at him, adoringly, waiting with floppy ears at attention like two pairs of silky pigtails.

What else could they do? Everyone aboard the *Compass Rose* couldn't help but like the dogs. Not just any dogs, but two of the most ridiculously cute little Golden Retrievers, about 3 or 4 months old.

Slinging a kitchen towel around his shoulders, Yeager moved forward and offered his hand to the dogs. "I hope you like stew." He smiled.

It was obvious that their canine lives had been disrupted, but they would be well cared for. They whined sometimes, a soft, plaintiff sound that spoke to their own distress. However, whenever the crew, particularly Will, came into sight, they wiggled and they yapped and leapt in the air. They were excited about these humans, and not just for the food that was offered to them.

Chapter 16

SOMETIMES HE FELT as if he was traveling through a long tunnel, sure that the end would never come.

As the brother of the proprietor of the *Compass Rose*, Will carried some authority, but Thomas Hale was still the captain.

The door to the dining room was huge and studded with brass. The entryway was draped with roses and vines, carved into the oak, starting above the door, reaching down almost to the deck's surface. Just above that was an enormous compass. Will took in a deep breath as he followed Captain Hale through the doorway.

Hale and Will began the daunting task of informing the crew - what they thought had happened to the crew of the schooner – and what was in store for their own crew.

"I'm not sure how to begin." Hale commanded their attention, but they continued talking and eating.

A troubled look passed over his face and his eyes moved along the faces at the table - a table that ran fore to aft, the entire length of the room. He cleared his throat in an attempt to gain their full attention. "I'm sure you are wondering why I called you here."

But they barely flicked a glance his way.

His typically friendly nature eclipsed by frustration and ire, he raised his voice. "I have learned that we may never find our way back to our homes." He passed his bottle to Yeager and he glanced at Will, pressing his lips in a tight, pale line.

Gasps and confusion erupted from the gathered crewmen. Then they all remained exactly where they stood, shrouded in silence.

Hale laughed, already visibly lighter, now that he had delivered the news. The spell broke and the barrage of endless questions began.

Will described what they had witnessed back aboard the schooner.

When he tried to explain to them that they were not actually dead *yet* because they have been assigned a task by the higher powers, whoever that is, *"to ... to ... well, we really don't know yet,"* another loud hush fell over the room. They stared back at him, in silence.

"Well I, for one, will be glad to get off this floating deathtrap, the first port we encounter!"

Will shook his head dismissively. "That's not possible. We are only permitted to go ashore within a predetermined distance from the *Compass Rose*."

Hale nodded in agreement. "He's right."

The questions continued and Captain Hale went over everything again. And then a third time. Where were they? Were they dead? If they weren't dead, why couldn't they go home? And why was there such a mystery surrounding what would happen to their souls if something happened and it wasn't their destined *time*.

And unfortunately, there were more questions than answers.

"Some of this is speculation. We really aren't sure."

"You made all of this up!" Morgan snorted.

"All we have to back anything up is the log." Hale held it up for them to see.

The crew crowded and rushed Hale to get at the log. The scene would have degenerated into complete lunacy if they had not a good script to follow. It had been prearranged that if they faced anything remotely resembling mutiny, Will would seize the log and lock it in the safe.

They went ballistic. Hale exchanged glances with Will. He dashed out and across the deck, tossing the book to him and shouted instructions.

Hale tried again without success to regain control, but they weren't having any of it. They backed him against the starboard rail. Hale's voice never wavered, but he was beginning to worry.

"Pow!"

Then again, *"Pop! … Bang!"*

The crew turned to find Will standing behind them, pistol poised high in the air. "Which one of you wants to find out if this is your time?"

Quiet again.

Will spoke again in a firm tone. "And don't think for one minute that I won't use this, if necessary." He put the pistol back in the holster hidden under his jacket

Morgan spat onto the deck, and looked back at Will. "Look at you! Aren't you afraid?"

"I don't think it's fear that I am struggling with," Will sighed. He walked toward him. "I am long over that sensation." He met Morgan, eye-to-eye, and continued his thought. "It's the uncertainty that has haunted me since the day we encountered that first, fateful storm."

"I'm too old for these shenanigans," Yeager mumbled under his breath. His knees snapped as he jumped to his feet. He guffawed and he took a swig from the flask. "Lies. Drunk liars only tell bigger tales."

Then, shaking off the reflective thought, he said, "Now, if you will excuse me, I have work to do."

But Yeager blocked Will from leaving. "We're as good as dead."

Will stared back at him, bringing his focus back to the deck, a dewy perspiration springing over his face. "Yeager, I wish it was all a big lie … but it isn't. It is all very real."

"Prove it!"

Will shouted up at the sky in exasperation. *"I wish I could!"*

Chapter 17

WILL WAS HURLED ten feet in the air. And then he landed with an eerie thud, on the deck. A portion of the crane that had mysteriously been ripped off its base landed on him, crippling his knees and shoulders.

He didn't move.

"Is he dead?" Yeager inquired.

Captain Hale turned his head in his direction and glared.

Yeager frowned, his mouth twisted as he thought. "Oh yeah," He scratched his head and mumbled, "Sorry."

Will woke to a sensation of pain. His lower back was screaming in agony. He tried to blink his eyes open, but they wouldn't. He heard voices, sounds, shuffling of feet. He struggled to lift his hand but he only got as far as wiggling his fingers.

Why was he lying on the deck? And why did he hurt so much?

"He's coming 'round." Will heard a relieved voice as if coming through a tunnel.

He was flat on his back, a kaleidoscope of light shifting around him. He jerked into a sitting position, but many hands restrained him. He tried to pull away.

The hands moved back to him and pushed him down. "Stockton." Hale said his name in the same tone you would with a skittish animal. "Look at me, Stockton."

Will recognized Hale's voice. "How many fingers do you see?"

"Fingers?" Will moaned.

"How many fingers am I holding up?" Captain Hale pulled in his thumb and held up his hand with the finger missing.

Will cleared his throat. "Three." His eyes adjusted to the light and he moved his fingers and his toes. He blinked and the blurriness left his vision.

The evening was warm and still. A tern flew over them, and disappeared back into the pink-tinged sky. They checked his vital signs and examined the deep gashes across his forehead.

The blood had instantly congealed. They gasped in disbelief.

Will felt oddly pleased with their reaction. It gave him validation - made his theory seem reasonable.

Out of the corner of his eye, he saw a vague claw of cloud reach toward him. He felt like a ghost … transparent … floating through time. He fell to the deck again, landing on his back.

Hale and Yeager rushed to Will and knelt beside him. The following moments were a blur, both familiar and peculiar.

He was alive.

Very much alive.

When he should be dead. He should have died.

But he was still there. Will's heart rate slowed. His breath came easier.

The roar of the ocean was hypnotic as he stared into the heavens, struggling to stand and regain his equilibrium again.

Hale took his hand with a warm grasp. "In life," he remarked when he helped Will to stand and patted him on the back, "maybe each person gets one or two miracles."

His expression softened and his eyes showed signs of an impending twinkle. "I believe you, my friend," he said, "just used one of yours."

WHILE HALE SIPPED the whiskey in hopes of settling his nerves, Will used the alcohol to dull the pain. He was disoriented and sore - the slightest effort to move sent a fresh stab of pain throughout his body.

Will blinked once, twice, and then recovered himself, shaking his head. "What in the hell are we going to do?"

"Let's not make too many plans right now," Captain Hale said, trying to make light of whatever had happened to them. "I think we've had enough excitement to last us for awhile."

Will leaned back on the chair and inhaled deeply. "I can't stop thinking about the legend," said Will. He made a useless attempt to clear his mind.

There was a knock at the door. Yeager appeared on the other side. Captain Hale sighed. "What is it, Yeager?"

Yeager bent down and picked up two scared little puppies. "You forgot someone." He smiled.

Will swept them from Yeager and held them up to his face. "They must have been so frightened!" Clancy licked his face and Hubble squirmed until he put them down. Clancy whimpered until he picked her back up.

Yeager, noticing the open box on the desk, walked over and scooped out a handful of the coins. He held it out to Thomas and Will in dismay. "This is gold! Have you ever seen anything like it?"

Clancy, whose natural curiosity had drawn her in, sniffed his hand and tried to lick them. Yeager chuckled. "It's nothing to eat, you silly dog." And he released the coins, watching them spill back into the box. He turned to Captain Hale and said, "We have to tell the crew about this, you know."

Hale dropped his jaw. "What? That would be crazy! They will kill us to get to it!"

"I suppose Yeager is right," Will said as he closed the box. "We have to be honest with them if we expect honesty in return. They will each get their fair share."

AS THE FIRST handful of crew members began to gather up their portion of the gold, one of them reminded the others of the passage William Stockton had read to them from the log. The last line in the book that read: *A man who picks up the stakes in greed, while abandoning ship will one day fall victim to the sea himself.*

Will stepped in and explained that, although they still possessed free will, they must think and make wise decisions. And that the consequences of not adhering to the guidelines would be dire.

They stilled. And the gold coins were voluntarily returned to the box.

Chapter 18

THE ANGRY SHOUTING of men's voices, twisting against each other making it difficult to decipher, jolted Will awake.

As he rose in alarm, they became muffled eerie echoes out on the water, then whispers, and then everything went silent. Will stood and his head spun. He pressed a hand to his forehead as if to hold his thoughts still.

Will hurried to the portside rail and looked over the edge, only to see two empty lifeboats, each with a bag of gold coins on one of its seats. He raised a hand to his unshaven chin and rubbed his stubble. The men were mysteriously absent.

Absent didn't begin to describe it.

THE MOON HUNG in the sky like a lantern and washed the surface of the *Compass Rose* in metallic light as all hands stood assembled before them.

Will had awakened Hale and, together, they roused the crew for the interrogation. But when they were asked what they knew about the lifeboats and the coins, the crew remained suspiciously silent.

Hale walked slowly along the row of ten men, counting, eying each one accusingly.

There were sixteen hands absent. He stopped and stared at the first mate. "You better start talking," he said. No response.

"Maybe I didn't make myself clear!" Hale boomed, leaning over and lifting him by the armpits. Then he turned and threw him into the stairwell leading to the engine room.

"I said …," he pointed to each of them. "… *Who were they?*"

An eerie feeling trickled throughout the *Compass Rose* as Will and the others began to realize that not only could they not remember their names, nobody could conjure up a picture of their faces. However, they were aware that something happened to somebody.

Hale frantically combed through the ship's manifest, but a chill ran down his spine when he read that *the Compass Rose* put to sea with only twelve hands aboard. Twelve men.

Nobody sets out on a voyage like this with only twelve hands! That would be insane!

"What do you think it means - them vanishing like that?"

The crew scrambled to the quarters where the men slept and kept their personal possessions, hoping for clues. However, not only were there no sea bags in their quarters … their bunks were gone. The beds in the sleeping quarters had been rearranged. Will walked through the compartments and counted.

Stunned silence reigned as this news was digested.

"Twelve – a mere dozen" Even though they knew for a fact that there had been twenty-eight.

Chapter 19

ILLNESS AND DEATH were two levels of loss; disappearance without explanation was another. There were nods and vague sounds of agreement among the ranks, but they clearly weren't sure exactly what had happened to the sixteen hands.

That evening, there was an awkward silence as they sat at the table. Will wondered if they were all thinking the same things he was - about the past, about the way small details add up to create an overwhelming wave. Happiness, tragedy, revenge - the outcomes of human actions were so difficult to predict and impossible to prevent.

The *Compass Rose* didn't have an official chaplain, but Emmett, the watchman, was the closest thing they had, since his father was an ordained Methodist minister back in his hometown of Ann Arbor, Michigan, and he had taken on the task of offering the nightly blessing at dinnertime.

"Well, at least we have our health," he finally said in an effort to lighten the moment. Everyone laughed, but as they raised their glasses in a toast to their new lives, they were all wondering how long it would take before the next unexpected turn of events shattered the fragile and temporary peace.

JIMMY SET HIS paintbrush down on the edge of the can and watched it teeter for a few moments then drop off onto the floor. He shook his head and spoke without emotion. "… painting the deck of a sinking ship."

With more than half of their crew gone, nonexistent or not, things had to change. Duties were reassigned, some completely eliminated.

Maintenance. Upkeep. Those were two of the things that were highly important to Captain Hale. The crew had rolled their eyes many times while listening to the captain sing the merits of keeping a tight ship. *"Maintenance paves the way to cleanliness. And cleanliness leads to pride."*

So it really didn't surprise them when Hale insisted the trim on the main deck receive a fresh coat of paint. Never mind that they weren't expecting company onboard, anytime soon.

They were secretly amused that the color of paint that had mysteriously appeared in the storeroom was rather "untraditional." Humor was something else they could count on to relieve some of the stress, and when they learned that orange was Captain Hale's least favorite color, they were covertly delighted to perform the task.

"Who in the hell thought this would be a good color?" Captain Hale boomed from the bridge deck. "And why, in God's name, is there nobody at the chadburn post?"

Morgan glanced up at him and said, "That is the color that was in the storeroom." He dipped his brush in the can and brought it out, dripping with the thick, flame-orange coating. "And there is nobody assigned to monitor the telegraph, sir." Which made perfect sense, since the telegraph didn't work anyway.

Concern among the ranks had been spreading that the crew size was not adequate for a ship the magnitude of the *Compass Rose*.

"We are a very small crew aboard the *Compass Rose*, indeed," Thomas Hale said as he pressed the bottle to his lips. "But then again, how big of a crew is necessary for a g*host ship*?" He laughed.

"Fine job, men." Will approached them from behind, holding an open book. He wanted to inquire as to the color choice, but he decided that, in light of so many other things that were out of place in their lives, a paint color was a minor disturbance.

Will addressed Captain Hale. "I have found a flaw in your theory …" He leaned against the rail, "… about the terns." As he talked, he became visibly distracted and bothered by a flying insect, buzzing his head. "We are on the lake." He pointed up at the flock of birds overhead. "So, you see … they can't be terns."

But Hale countered. "Terns nest on rocky islands, barrier beaches, and saltmarshes and forage over open waters including inlets, lakes, and marine waters. During the breeding season they frequent both salt and freshwater."

The fly made an attempt to avoid Will's hand, and over calculated, landing in the wet paint on the ledge under the rail. It struggled, but was finally able to escape to the other side of the deck.

"Haven't you had enough of that log, Stockton?" Pointing to the book in Will's hand, Hale added, "Surely by now you know everything there is to know."

Will shut the book and held it up for Captain Hale to see. "This is not the log, Thomas."

Hale swiped the book from his hand and opened it. "Sherlock Holmes." He stroked his beard. "Ah yes … the story I studied once in school, about the British investigator and his sidekick."

He handed the book back to Will. "It's been quite some time since I read this."

The fly hummed Will again. "Blasted insect! I have no food, but it refuses to leave me alone!" Will continued to track it. It suddenly landed on the open splay of the book.

Hale laughed. "Look – we have a fly who likes to read!" And he handed the book back to Will.

The fly flew off during the transfer of the book, and lit on the edge of a chair. Will opened it and paged through the beginning. The fly buzzed him incessantly again and landed on the first page of chapter two.

"We are not unlike the characters in this book, you know, Stockton," Hale said. "Our experiences aboard the *Compass Rose* have been very similar to investigations, haven't they?"

"But why is it that we always seem to wind up with more questions than answers?" Will watched the fly light on Hale's shoulder.

Hale said, "I suppose one could draw a comparison between Sherlock Holmes and our plight. He was known for his prowess at using logic and astute observation to solve cases, wasn't he?"

He leaned in and chuckled. "Trouble is, which one of us is Holmes?"

Will popped the pesky fly with the closed book, while it sat on Hale's shoulder. Then he leaned in and flicked the dead fly off onto the floor grates. He looked down at it, shaking his head. He grinned.

"Sorry, my dear Watson."

Chapter 20

CAPTAIN HALE SUCCESSFULLY blew a smaller smoke ring through a larger one. He leaned forward and patted Hubble and Clancy on their heads. "Did you see that?"

"Well *I* certainly did," countered Will, who was coming down from the bridge deck.

Hale continued to hold his canine audience captive. "If you'd learn to smoke, I could teach you all kinds of tricks. Watch this." Clancy jumped as he exhaled a vertical loop that quickly disappeared after sucking it back into his mouth." Both dogs were intrigued, but Clancy was mesmerized.

"For God's sake," said Will. "Get back on topic! If we don't figure this out, we are destined to wander forever."

Hubble yawned and settled onto a pile of blankets for a long afternoon nap, while Clancy took off, chasing after anything that moved on the deck and in the air.

Dark clouds were moving in with a gusty wind, the storm seeming to approach ever closer, just as Hale had predicted.

Will saw whitecaps forming on tips of the choppy, turbulent water. "I don't like the look of those clouds." He frowned at the sky. "Seems whenever those fronts start picking up speed, we are in for another surprise."

Clancy began making a ruckus out on the deck and Will ran to investigate. She was chasing tiny bits of debris across the surface of the floor planks. Will talked to her, but he stopped mid-sentence as he noticed wings with tiny specks of orange fly past his eyes. They buzzed him, creating such an annoyance around Will's head that he reached out and swatted at them with his hand when they landed on the back of a deck chair. The fly dropped to the deck.

Will chuckled and made a comment about how flies annoy him more than just about anything. "That'll teach you!"

Chapter 21

ON THEIR BEST days, they felt blessed to have had it all. On the worst days, they felt cheated that they had lost it so soon.

Will occupied much of his time making the rounds, soaking up as much knowledge as he could, learning all he could about the *Compass Rose*.

Will studied the fireman's face as his eyes darted around the engine room. Although it was lit, Will realized how dingy the space really was. The single bulb hanging from the ceiling barely created enough light to see what he was doing.

It was the job of the fireman, assisted by the coal passer, to keep the furnaces fired. They worked in the fire hold, where the normal temperature sometimes reached 120 degrees or more, moving the coal.

Firing a coal furnace was an art. Using the coal shovel, the fireman would close the damper, open the firing door, scoop up a shovel full of coal, lift, pivot, and swing the shovel to spray the coal evenly over the fire, close the firing door, and open the damper - all-in-one continuous motion. The performance could easily have been set to music.

If he forgot to close the damper before adding coal, flames would leap out the firing door and singe him. Boiler pressure was regulated by controlling the amount of coal being burned, and by adjusting the dampers. If the boiler had a full head of steam going and Captain Hale ordered the vessel to slow down or stop, the fireman had to get the boiler pressure down as quickly as possible by pulling the fires. That meant shoveling burning coal back out of the furnace on to the fire hold deck.

The main job of a coal passer was to bring coal to the fire hold in a wheelbarrow from the coal bunker where hundreds of tons of it was stored.

He found a warm, comfortable spot on the floor grates of the engine room, leaning against a locker and, after combing through the pages of the log again, Will fell asleep. An hour later, the sound of coal rushing down the shoot awakened him. He blinked.

"I don't know why you are so fixated on that log, Will. In time, I suppose we will learn to accept it as a natural order, like the journey of the stars," Captain Hale said to Will, leaning over him.

Will picked up the log resting next to him and opened it just long enough to let out a short laugh. "I find that hard to believe. Just when I think I have one thing figured out, I come across an entry in this book that raises yet another question ..." he quickly rested the book in his lap and stopped mid-sentence, his eyes catching something behind Yeager, who was approaching them with a pan of biscuits.

When he said nothing else, Hale glanced at Will. His eyes were wide, unblinking, and he followed the direction of his gaze. It was fixed on the air above Yeager, following something that apparently was moving towards them. Will jumped up and grabbed Yeager's arm.

There was a housefly hovering above Yeager's head, close enough that he could see the texture of its wings. He watched it fly higher, forming an arc, but not before Will noticed the tiny flash of bright orange on its wings. It dove back to eye level, and it sat on the open page of the journal, on the floor.

Will sat silently and studied the insect closely. Then, he slowly opened his fingers and turned his palm upward. The fly landed squarely in his palm.

What were the odds?

But before he had time to give it much more contemplation than that, Thomas reached around from behind him and, with a swift swat, the fly was history.

Well, of course it was ridiculous. It was one thing to have faith in the unknown and unseeable, and to have debates about theories such as the existence of a god or atheism. It was one thing to decide if you believe in time travel or guardian angels or the difference between coincidence and synchronicity.

But to believe for even a moment that a dead fly had just flown through the door to the engine room, after having been killed twice, also not particularly interested in food, possessing a high degree of intelligence and attempting to get his attention - well, let's face it, that's neither faith nor science - it's just plain crazy.

Chapter 22

AT NIGHTFALL, THEY were still sitting in the captain's dining hall, finishing their supper, which had consisted of what Yeager called *peasant food* – carrot stew and a light, unsalted bread.

"Quiet!" Will said as he blew out the candle, leaving them in total darkness. A sliver of moonlight made its way between the slats of the shutters painting fine lines across the floorboards. "Did you hear that?"

Hale set down his fork and boomed, "Hear what?"

Captain Hale stood, but Will held up his hand. "Shhhh … I'll go outside and investigate."

Fear made them obedient. Hale sat straight back in his chair. And as the sudden hush fell over the cabin, Will cracked the door, then silently tiptoed out onto the deck.

He wished he had his pistol as he walked slowly around the perimeter of the deck, his eyes searching the obscurity.

Ears straining, eyes trying to see in the darkness, Will crept along, counting his heartbeats, ready to lunge. But there was no sound but the lapping of the waves against the hull of the ship.

His eyes were drawn to the quarterdeck as he began to sense that he was being observed. He squinted in the moonlight and could make out a dark figure moving around - a shadowy figure ducking in and out of his line of sight.

Will began the climb up. He moved fast, smoothly, every step springy and catlike. His foot searched beyond the first rung of the iron ladder that ascended up to the weather deck.

From above, his light shone into the blackness below. A silhouette passed by the base of the ladder he was on. He held his breath and waited until the coast was clear before continuing.

But he only reached half way up the ladder before a bullet whizzed past his head, grazing his cheek. It came from the main deck, where he had just been. He strained his eyes and made out the faint outline of the perpetrator through the moonlight - a tall, lanky man. He sensed pure evil emanating from him.

Will launched off the rung and flew through the air, landing on the man, knocking him to the deck. He covered him completely. A struggle quickly ensued. Will was more interested in restraint, but his attacker seemed hell-bent on the offensive, pounding him with fists.

He found the man's style of fighting a bit odd, and embarrassingly easy to overthrow. Having been professionally trained in boxing while attending college in Ireland, Will found himself more concerned about not doing the man more harm than necessary. That concern dissipated the moment his groin was introduced to a boot. The wailing of his groan echoed across the surface of the *Compass Rose.*

The crew, waiting silently in the officer's dining room, winced and cringed as they listened to Will's cry of agony, imagining the excruciatingly horrible fate he was meeting out on the deck alone.

Hale sprang up, flung open the door and darted out into the dark, followed closely by Morgan and Yeager.

Will doubled over but quickly recovered and swiftly grabbed the man's wrists, pinning them over his head. Concern flashed across his face when he realized that the man was not a man at all. Abruptly, his hands stopped on hers. He did a theatrical double-take.

"This can't be. I must be losing my mind."

Grayish eyes, framed by the leather flaps of an aviator's cap flashed angrily up at him.

Will had never been one to follow women's fashion, but he did find hats to be of particular interest. Growing up, he had been fascinated and curious as to why the millinery profession seemed to be obsessed with feathers -- so many at times, that a good gust of wind might send its wearer flying. It was intriguing how they stopped each other on the street to fuss and chat about them. To him, women's hat trends served no practical purpose whatsoever.

But hers was a leather helmet - a flying cap. And goggles to boot.

"Do you always talk to yourself?" she asked him, with sarcasm in her voice.

He studied her. She was attractive, in an ordinary way - windswept hair, with a slender, boyish figure.

She turned her head to study his profile. A gentle face that came together pleasingly. But from that angle, she couldn't see his eyes.

There was a drawn-out moment of disturbed silence. Waves beat out their rhythm on the hull as the moon slipped from behind the clouds and lit the deck of the *Compass Rose* below.

"What's *wrong* with you?" he asked, annoyed. He helped her up.

"*Me?* What's wrong with *me?*" She threw back. "You're not the one who found herself suffocating under the weight of a strange man.

Will couldn't find the words to speak.

She pulled the cap off her head and glared at him. "Well, sir ..." She huffed, hesitated and drew in a long breath, exhaling in anger as the rest of the words spewed from her mouth, taking Will by surprise ... " your ship nearly capsized my vessel. I am certain you are breaking some kind of maritime law. Make no mistake; I shall report you to the authorities on my return!" The way she said it made it sound almost scientific.

Will stood and brushed the debris from his trousers. The corners of his lips deepened. "You look like you're going to take a swing at me."

She frowned. "I'm tempted."

PUTTING HIS FINGER to his lips, Thomas moved toward the stern, grabbing a line he could use to restrain Will's perpetrator. Before they'd gone more than a few steps, they spotted the two figures.

It was dark, but she sensed their presence. She turned and glared at the surprised men staring at them, open-mouthed. "Well, this is a fine how-do-you-do, if I don't mind saying so."

Will's cheeks reddened slightly.

"What's a woman doing on this boat?" Yeager asked Hale.

"Guess we'll find out in a couple minutes," he said.

She moved carefully along the deck, watching her footing and matching her steps to the roll of the boat until she was face-to-face with Thomas Hale.

"Who are you?"

"The captain of this ship," said Hale as he looped the line around a deck cleat and stared back at the woman. "Who are you?" he demanded.

Of course, they would know all about her. She had come to fame, with her highly-publicized flight around the world. They read the papers.

She stammered a little, not sure how to respond. It seemed like everywhere she went, flash powder was exploding all around her. She could feel the crowds pressing closer and closer. Sometimes she felt like an animal trapped, surrounded by people and reporters and photographers. Especially that last year - 1937.

So she decided, since they hadn't recognized her yet, that she would not reveal her identity. After all, it would just be a matter of time.

Thinking quickly, she was able to form words on her lips. She shivered in the cold. "…I - I'm … Milly."

Will took off his jacket and placed it around her shoulders. "Good to meet you, Milly. Though I wish that you had not exploded on the scene with such enthusiasm."

She slowly slid to a sitting position and she looked up at Will, the fight in her eyes dwindling. "Where am I?"

He smiled at the ironic question. Even *he* didn't know where they were. Only that they were on the *Compass Rose*.

"Milly …" Will began as he squatted to her level. "What do you remember? About what happened to you before you came aboard our ship?"

She rubbed her head. "I was on the final leg of a flight around the world, when something went horribly wrong."

Yeager leaned into Will and murmured, "I'll say."

She looked around, rattled. "My raft! Where's my raft?"

But when they peered over the sides of the ship, they didn't see a raft.

Captain Hale looked confused. "You tried to fly around the world, in a raft? What in hell are you talking about, Susie?"

Yeager threw in his two cents worth, infusing the moment with a touch of humor. "Actually, I think she flew in a plane."

But Will shushed him, listening to her with interest. Her eyes slid closed. "We're losing her … *Good God* –would somebody get the girl some water?" She misted over and Will caught her as she swayed in the frigid, night air.

Morgan rushed over with a canteen and placed the open vessel in her hands. She held it, but she was too weak to lift it. Will took her hands and guided them, but he only got as high as her chin before the water spilled from the canteen.

She began to drop off again. Will cradled her head until she was at the right position. And he poured the water, some actually reaching her mouth. She swallowed, and then she gave a little cough.

"I have been floating in the darkness, bobbing along the waves. I waited, in rain falling from a sky that had no end." She closed her eyes and opened them again. "I sat … and I drifted."

Hale inquired, "How long have you been out there, Susie?"

"Two days - maybe three." She inhaled deeply. "I tossed for such a long while. At times, I thought I saw tiny faint lights in the distance, but the waves had carried me too far to tell. I was too tired to think." Will helped her as she struggled to sit upright. "Never have I felt so drowsy. I had lost all hope."

Will and the others leaned in, as Milly's voice lowered in volume, almost impossible to hear her.

"Then I saw something. I was afraid to allow myself to think that a boat might be coming, I blinked. It was still there." She drifted and her eyes illuminated while she relived the memory. "Yes. It was coming closer, cutting through the water toward me, gradually becoming brighter." She pulled the jacket tighter against her body.

The crew waited for her to finish.

"Light."

Will smiled and nodded. "The *Compass Rose*."

Just before she closed her eyes again, she strained to turn her head and looked over at Captain Hale. With a definite edge to her voice, she spoke to him. "And stop calling me *Susie*. The name is Milly. I would appreciate it if you would respect that."

Chapter 23

WILL DETERMINED THAT the quarters he had been staying in were the only place he felt comfortable having a woman, all by herself on a ship, among a dozen men, sleeping in.

Being fairly certain she wouldn't want to share the space with him, Will showed Milly to what would be her quarters - his spacious owner's stateroom, which was separated from the guest staterooms and captain's quarters by a small lounge.

He smiled. The last person he'd had to share a room with, his last bunkmate, back home on the farm in Illinois, was his brother John.

They really hadn't needed to share a room - there were other empty rooms in the house - but Will liked the idea of having someone nearby as he fell asleep, and John liked having someone else in his room. There had been no argument as to who would sleep where - John wanted the bottom bunk so he could pretend he was sailing on the ocean. He had tucked a sheet into the corners of the mattress above, making it drape down like a ship's sail.

And Will had been delighted being on the top bunk so he could pretend he was on a wing of an airplane or the highest deck of a spaceship. He used to draw stars on the ceiling of the room for the sky.

"Let's get you settled. You'll feel better in a moment," he assured her as he directed her to what would be her quarters.

Her heart warmed at his words. Could she trust him? Who knew? But at least, for the moment, he seemed sincere and that alone brought a lump to her throat - made her feel close to a man she barely knew.

"If I take your room, where will you stay?"

He gathered his things and explained to her, "I will be moving into a hall forward cabin, near the radio room."

"I can stay in a smaller cabin - really I can."

"It will be fine. Actually, it's one of the few cabins with its own bathroom - one of the rooms that has become recently vacant." He said nothing about their *historical rewrite* and how the cabins had become vacant.

"Thank you." She wrapped her arms around her waist as though she were cold. "I still can't believe it."

"Is this too much air for you? I can close the window." Will leaned over her to close the porthole.

"No. Actually, the breeze feels good." Milly settled onto the bed and stared out the porthole, deep in thought. She interrupted her own thoughts. "Would you stay with me? For just a little while?"

Will set his gear back on the floor and realized that he had been just about the only one who had spoken much to her. Of course, she was curious ... probably frightened.

"Where am I?"

He sat next to Milly on the bed and he let out a nervous laugh. "You're not going to believe me." He leaned in closer. "Where would you like me to start?"

It took a long hour for him to explain their rather unique predicament to Milly. He told her of the hurricane. "One moment, I saw the sea, rolling, swallowing us like it was alive, and the next thing nothing. Rain, dark sky, nothing, rain, dark sky, nothing and finally, just nothing."

Milly watched his eyes as he continued.

"The way the sea was raging on," he said, "It looked like the *Compass Rose* would soon join its predecessors, in *Davy Jones's Locker*. We knew something had to be done fast."

Then Will went on to tell Milly about the day he had witnessed, first-hand, one of the keys to how they were mysteriously transported through time and space. He paused. "And then ... we took a flying turn into the storm clouds."

He described the clipper ship they found and of the demise of her crew. Milly's eyes widened as he talked about the missing members from their own vessel, the *Compass Rose*.

"They must have been crazy, Will!"

"Crazy's normal around here," he said, and she half—laughed, even though deep in her heart, she knew he was probably right.

"Where did they go? What happened to them?" she asked Will.

"We left them in the dust…" he paused and then with a smile, he finished, "… so to speak."

"Greed is such an awful motive, isn't it?"

CLANCY AND HUBBLE were waiting patiently outside the door when Will stepped out onto the deck. Milly laughed at the confused look on their faces. "Aren't you two of the sweetest little faces I have ever seen?" She looked up at Will and went on. "They are almost identical, aren't they? If one of them wasn't so much larger than the other one, I wouldn't be able to tell them apart."

After Will explained where they came from, she leaned down and said, "You poor little orphans."

Chapter 24

SHE CLIMBED UP higher and at the top, she was staring at the great expanse of the ocean.

After all but the night crew had retired, Will went out to count the stars from the weather deck. On his approach, he was surprised to find Milly there, staring up into the midnight sky.

It startled him for a moment to see her there, gripping the rail with both hands. The rain that had been pelting earlier had subsided, leaving a soft mist that seemed to thicken the air. The moon lit the waves in her hair better than any light bulb ever could.

Neither one said anything as they stood, side-by-side, sharing the view. The wind played on his face as he traced the constellations with his eyes.

"My dream has always been to conquer the sky."

She faced him. "Are you a pilot?"

He shook his head slowly and let out a little chuckle of irony. "No. I guess it just wasn't in the stars, so to speak."

Will went on to explain why he was on the *Compass Rose,* about his brother, and that life on the water had never been part of his plan.

"I was disappointed, of course, but I have read tales of times when ships navigate the sky." He looked at Milly and winked. "So, in a roundabout way, I suppose I am living my dream. I have found sailing to be quite a challenge. It's all about the curve of the wind and the velocity, you know."

"How old are you, Will?"

In the midst of all his questions and confusion, Will wasn't really sure. The more he thought about it, in the end, it was just another day - - he supposed he must have reached a milestone somewhere along the way. Some time during the past days, he supposed he had turned 36. Or at least he thought so.

That night, Milly lay on the cusp of sleep, but sleepless, for a long time that night. Her eyes gazed at the ceiling, looking at nothing, watching only shimmering shapes as clouds disturbed the moonlight.

WILL SETTLED IN for the evening. He glanced across the cabin at the vast library, consisting of five books, all of which he'd already read. Which one would it be tonight?

The walls rattled briefly as a strong wind passed over the *Compass Rose*. Will cast his eyes around the room uncomfortably, then lit on a tiny orange fleck, resting on a book, laying on the dresser. He stepped closer and picked up the orange-tipped, dead fly with the edge of a rolling paper.

"Watson. Is that you?" He studied the carcass closely, then he carefully put it back down on the book again and turned around. But he spun back.

"I'm not crazy," Will said to the fly. "And I won't let you, or anyone else, convince me that I am."

He went to his bed, reaching under the mattress with another suspicious glance at the fly, unexpectedly feeling watched." He took out the book he had hidden there, and sat back on the bed, opening it to the place he had left off.

Will closed the book, trying to rationalize for a moment, the situation. "I'm not crazy," he spoke to the fly again. "I know what I saw."

And as he drifted off to sleep, he thought he heard the sound again - a whirring, a buzzing, and then silence.

IN THE MORNING, Watson was gone.

Chapter 25

MILLY WATCHED THE dogs chase after a tern that had landed on the deck to devour crumbs left over from breakfast.

The morning sky was a brilliant autumnal blue, washed clean. She felt dumbstruck as she paced the portside deck of the *Compass Rose*.

It wasn't that she was ungrateful for the rescue, or that she wasn't happy to have people to talk to again … to interact with. The trouble was that she had begun to believe that the only person who wasn't losing all of his marbles on this ship was William. Everyone else, from the cook, to the steward to the fireman to the crane operator to the first mate and of course, Captain Hale, didn't seem to be completely together. Was there an engineer or a mechanic? Nobody seemed to ever be actually working.

Didn't anyone have a job?

ONE BY ONE, the man hoisted wooden crates from one side of the deck to the stairs leading below. When he returned to the main deck, he was surprised to see Milly standing very close to the deck crane, studying it carefully.

Will rounded the corner just in time to warn her. Milly turned and faced Will. He stopped next to her and he pulled her back. "Don't get too close!"

The sarcastic snort emanating from the man's mouth said it all. She caught a spark in Will's eye as the two men exchanged a look of humor.

"Who are you?" she asked.

Will answered for him. "Ernie is our Steward." He paused and continued. "And our crane operator."

She walked past Will and closer to Ernie. She gave him a smile. "Ernie -- What are you doing?"

"Restocking ammunition, ma'am."

Milly turned to Will with a look of confusion. He smiled at her as he guided her to the portside rail.

"Why would anyone here need to restock ammunition?" She hesitated for a moment and finished the question in a voice just above a whisper. "And where, pray-tell, does he get it from?"

"We get just what we need. No more, no less."

"Will – are you telling me that ….. How is that possible?"

He gazed out over to where the water met the sky. He took a deep breath and then he let it out. "If I had the answer to that, I would also know why the sun still comes up every day, regardless of what atrocity has happened the day before. We surface a little worse for the wear, but nonetheless, we are here. We exist – for what, nobody knows."

"It appears every morning, so it must be needed." He pointed. "And tomorrow it will be gone, only to appear on the deck again."

"When?"

He checked his pocket watch. "Oh, about 7 O'clock. Or 8 … maybe 10. Who knows what time it is?"

"But why do you say that it is needed?"

"We aren't sure. But we have learned that we are only given what we need - nothing more, nothing less."

Milly stared up at Will, in dumbfounded silence. She looked so confused that Will couldn't help himself from smiling. It was like laughing in church. You know you shouldn't, but once you start, you can't stop.

He said it with a straight face, but there was a hint of amusement in his voice. "It does take some getting used to."

Chapter 26

CRASH!

His muscles gripped like a vise down his neck, reaching out like a triangle of pain. Ernie, the crane operator had made a miscalculation - a mistake that should have stripped William Stockton of a valuable worldly possession -- his existence. The heavy equipment had toppled over, pinning Will underneath.

Ernie, Hale and Morgan flew to the scene, along with anyone else who could leave their post.

Milly, once she got over the initial shock of what had just happened, ran to his aid, astonished that he was still conscious.

"Does this hurt?" She reached to touch the gash just above an even deeper wound.

"A little bit." Will winced and tried to retract his leg. "Don't." He flinched and then he looked back at her. "We have someone on the crew, not a doctor, but a man who is trained in medical ways. His name is Casey." He struggled to sit up.

But Milly stopped him. "Stop being so difficult, Will! I trained in medicine at Columbia University. And …," her voice intensified, "I was an army nurse in '18, during the war." She finished her thought. "You don't have anything I haven't seen before." But her eyes widened.

Milly watched her fingers coat themselves with blood, then fade into his skin as she touched the lesion, only to reappear as she pulled back her hand. The blood was gone. She felt her jaw drop. Suddenly her face contorted.

He swallowed hard. "I bruise; I bleed; I feel pain. But tomorrow, there will be little or no trace of it." He cringed again." Some of the pain remains for a few days, but the danger disappears."

Milly's eyes widened. "But how is that possible?"

Will struggled, against Milly's wishes, but he managed to stand up. He groaned and leaned back over, as the pain seemed to rip his leg in two.

"I don't know." he said, gasping. "Most of the time, we try to be tough and resilient." He inclined his head, and then he stared at her. "Truth is we don't have all the answers." He glanced away, then back again. "Hell, we don't have *any* of the answers!"

"When will it happen to you - how will you know when it's your time?" Milly probed. "Your *real time*?"

"We don't know ... maybe we will never know. But that's why it's important to live every day out here as if it could be our last."

With Milly on one side and Hale along the other, Will hobbled, wincing and grimacing, back to his cabin. He refused to allow them into the compartment. The moment they turned to leave, he shut the door -- and he passed out on the floor.

Chapter 27

ANOTHER DAY PASSED before Will felt strong enough to venture out of his quarters. Between the efforts of Milly and Yeager, he had been well-nourished, but he missed the fresh air.

Later that night, Milly assessed the darkness surrounding her and took a deep breath before knocking on Will's door, bracing herself for his initial reaction.

The knock broke Will's concentration. He looked through the peephole. Milly stood on the other side, holding a briefcase.

"William," she said when the door opened. She gave the humble interior of the cabin a sad glance. "I'd like to speak with you, if you have a minute."

Milly didn't wait to be invited in. She pushed past him and sat on the bunk, holding the satchel on her lap. She eyed her surroundings, surveying the cramped compartment, feeling guilty that he had given up his spacious quarters when she joined them. She looked up at him. "Nice place."

"I suppose - if you're a hobo."

"I have something to show you."

He shrugged with no expression.

Milly patted the spot next to her on the bed. "Sit."

He stepped closer and stopped. He didn't sit down.

"Will - I want you to promise me that you will not be upset with what I am going to show you." She unbuckled the case, lifted out a drawstring bag and reached inside.

She handed him a newspaper, just as a pesky fly buzzed around his head. He instinctively rolled the paper and swatted it. It dropped to the floor, deader than a doornail.

"Poor little fly ...," Milly sighed, "... such a short life." She retrieved the newspaper off the floor and handed it back to Will.

"You're worried about a fly?" He eyed Milly as he swiped the paper from her.

"Oh, I don't know." She stared at the motionless carcass, laying on the cabin floor. "I guess I feel sorry for the little thing."

Will rattled the pages as he attempted to put the newspaper back in order. "Well, don't."

"I know - it's rather silly, isn't it?"

Will started from the back page of the paper, quickly flipping through it as he continued. "He'll be back."

"Excuse me?"

"I said he'll be back."

Milly thought Will had lost his mind. She stared back at him in silence.

He placed the newspaper in his lap, shook his head and smiled at her. "That's Watson." Then he bent down and scraped up the lifeless corpse with the paper. "He has a real mischievous way about him. If he wants something from me, he finds an indirect way to get it."

"You named a dead fly?"

"Not just any dead fly. Watson is our resident *house fly*."

Milly sat on the cot with a thump. She put her head in her hands. *Could this situation get any weirder?*

"We have an understanding." He smiled at her. "I've grown rather fond of him. He's actually quite low-maintenance -- doesn't eat much."

She interrupted him. "But, Will ..."

"Every day he annoys me and I swat him."

"I know. I saw you kill him."

"And the next day, he's back."

WILL PICKED UP the newspaper again and opened it. Then he quickly went back to the front page and he froze.

The headline read:

MISS EARHART STARTS WORLD FLIGHT-FINAL EDITION

He thought out loud. *The Cleveland Plain Dealer?*

Milly watched his expression and explained. "It was given to me by a man from Cleveland, while I was in Honolulu."

He laughed as he turned the page of the newspaper again, in disbelief. He paused to read a few words.

Will's eyebrows slid up to his hairline.

"Milly,' he said, then flipped the paper back to look at the front page again. "You're a magician," he said with a grin.

Milly interrupted him. "Will, I am no magician. This is for real."

"Let's see ..." eyes moving rapidly over the lines as he ran his finger slowly down to the middle of the page. He stopped. Milly studied his face, for what, she didn't know.

"1937?" Will quickly flipped back to the front page again and repeated himself. *"1937?"*

He jumped up like he'd seen a ghost, the *Plain Dealer* hitting the deck. "This is preposterous."

"That's understandable," Milly answered in a soft, cultured tone.

Will inundated his new friend with history questions. What had happened in the world between September 1926 and ... 1937?

Will listened intently while Milly told him about the stock market crash of '29.

"So I should be glad I didn't invest my *vast wealth* in the market?" He gave her a slantwise grin full of charm.

Milly made a face, hugging the newspaper over her heart. She did her best to answer the many questions he had.

How could she explain it when she really didn't understand it herself?

Chapter 28

A HURRICANE WAS not a run-of-the-mill occurrence for the *Compass Rose* - there was always the chance that this could be the one that would do them all in. But with each impending storm, the sense of urgency weakened.

Terns called from somewhere above her head, and late evening shadows chilled her arms.

It was closing in on midnight now, and the breeze blowing on the deck made her wish she'd borrowed a heavier jacket from the closet. Milly caught up with Will, Hubble and Clancy on their nightly walk.

The sky was clear, the moon half full, stars glittering like scattered diamonds.

"Wish upon a star?" she asked.

From behind, they must have looked like the perfect couple. It might have been romantic... if they hadn't been standing in between the pages of time.

She jumped when a gull - or some other seabird with a wide wingspan - whooshed across, directly in front of her. Then feeling foolish over her jumping, she laughed with self-deprecation. "Birds are not usually something that scare me."

Will turned to face her and took in a deep breath. "I would like to tell you a story about a special kind of bird out here." He brought out a small flask from the inside pocket of his coat, and passed it to her, but she declined it.

His jaw tightened. "Milly, I think you're going to need this."

SHE DRANK FROM the bottle but left the last little bit for him. Will finished the rest and recapped the empty flask. The world tilted, just a bit, and she lost her center.

"Terns?" she squinted one eye and asked again.

Will didn't elaborate. His expression didn't change. He nodded and repeated himself. "Yes. *Flying* Terns."

Chapter 29

BY MIDMORNING, YEAGER was already in a foul mood.

Yeager. He held a special place in their hearts, and he loved nothing better than to argue with everybody, regardless of who was right or wrong. And although he was the only cook aboard for this voyage, the man insisted on being called the first-cook.

Women. Yeager threw his hands up in the air, just as Will rounded the turn.

Milly wasn't particularly fond of Yeager -- and for some reason, he didn't like her very much either.

There was a part of Yeager's brain that counted. It counted, whether he wanted it to or not. He couldn't help it. He was twenty-three years older than Thomas Hale. There were exactly eight steps from the galley doorway to the stove. Unless they were small steps - in that case there were twelve. They had been out to sea for only four days when their lives changed forever. There were thirty-six bowls in the cupboard.

And yesterday, there were exactly fourteen cans of beans on the pantry shelf.

He had only meant to walk past the pantry on his way out the door, but he stopped dead in his tracks when his peripheral vision sent him a signal. Something was amiss.

There were only twelve cans of beans on the pantry shelf. Which meant that there were exactly two missing!

And he had seen that woman secretly rummaging through his pots the day before.

She's behind this!

"Yeager! What's for supper?" He was startled back to reality with the sound of Will's voice, coming from the deck behind him.

Yeager felt the heat of anger creeping up the sides of his neck as he conjured up the image of Milly, secretly stealing his precious cans of beans.

"Stockton - you are nothing more than a marionette, and that woman pulls your strings." He frowned and disappeared into the galley.

Will had to admit, Milly was a distraction. But not so much that she interfered with their daily routine.

YEAGER'S WHISPERED CURSE floated around the noisy kitchen.

She stood, peeling, chopping and taking vengeance on a large onion, when he approached her.

"I want to know how you got directed to my boat."

"So do I, said Milly." She bit her lip and she went on. "I made something different today – surely they must be tired of the same thing day after day."

Milly was intimidated by the onion, though she had chopped dozens before, and afraid that the one correct way of doing this would, of course, escape her - in front of that insufferable man. It was as if she were handling a knife for the very first time. Her fingers meticulously worked the onion skin, and she chopped the bulb in quarters before getting down to business.

Then she turned and met his eyes. "And I do not believe this ship belongs to you."

"This kitchen does."

She pushed past him and began dicing a carrot.

Yeager lifted a snowy eyebrow. "What are you doing here then? Who are you?" he demanded.

Fumes from the onions stung her eyes, but they were watering anyway. "Through no choice of my own, of all the vessels on the seas,

I ended up on your wretched barge a week ago, and I wish I had walked out of your stinking kitchen the moment I set foot in it!"

Yeager took a step back, insulted by the affront. "It's not a barge and my kitchen doesn't stink," he said. "And it's in pristine condition - at least it was until... "

"Don't you dare say what I think you are about to say!" said Milly, holding the knife in the air.

Yeager peered dubiously into the stew pot. In his saltiest voice, he asked, "What's that floating on the top?"

She turned, knife in her hand. "Spinach."

"*Spinach?* How did you get spinach?"

She replied with a smug grin. "I asked for it."

His mouth dropped open in disbelief. Of all the times he had complained and scowled about the lack of ingredients to make something different, each morning he was met with the exact same fresh produce in the galley. Potatoes, carrots, celery, onion and green beans.

Milly saw the dismay written across Yeager's face. She wiped her hands on the apron – *his apron*, and joined him at the stove. She smiled and quietly said one word. *"Politely."* And she handed him the apron and walked out of the galley.

Yeager made a gagging sound, dropped the lid back on the pot and scowled. He was afraid to ask what else was in it.

Milly smiled as she opened the door to her cabin. She felt she had made some ground with the insufferable man.

Now all she had to do was go back in there and stand up for her rights.

Maybe tomorrow.

Chapter 30

NO ONE OTHER than the dogs seemed to appreciate the wonderful day as they raced up and down the deck, chasing each other. Both puppies seemed to bloom under all the attention they were getting from the crew.

They were so rambunctious that they actually ran off the end of the starboard side, tumbling into the water below.

Will saw it from the bridge and vaulted down the steps to the deck where they had fallen. He ran to the railing and searched for the puppies. He breathed a sigh of relief as he watched the two little heads pop up to the water's surface.

Assisted by Milly, he manned a lifeboat and set out on a short rescue mission. Neither dog resisted as they pulled them into the lifeboat. They reached and handed them, one at a time, to the waiting crew of the *Compass Rose*.

As Will and Milly attempted to dry them off, Clancy's tail wagged so hard, Will thought she might fling it off. Even after she was relatively dry, she chose to stay close to Will.

Hubble was too busy having fun, romping around the ship. Milly laughed as she sat next to Clancy, who had been sunning herself on the deck. She twined her fingers into Clancy's coat.

Of the two, Clancy was definitely experiencing more difficulty getting acclimated. She clearly loved the crew, but Will thought she seemed distant at times, easily distracted, often staring off into the ocean, almost as if she was searching for something.

Chapter 31

THE SUN BEGAN its slow descent, drenching the deck with suggestions of amethyst and magenta.

Thomas approached Will, dragging two collapsible chairs behind him. "Glad the pups are okay." Hale unfolded each and gestured for Will to have a seat in the one closest to him. Then he sat, facing Will and took in a deep breath. As he exhaled, he spoke. "I have a revelation, Stockton."

"What do you mean?" Will asked him.

"For whatever reason, something happened to us – something we don't understand. It's almost as if time just stopped for us all."

Will's eyes shifted over to Clancy, snoozing, curled up alongside Hubble, her paws dwarfing his by almost double. She felt his gaze and opened one eye. She rose and totted over to Will, sensing his concern. He scratched her behind her ears and smiled. He looked back at Hale.

Hale followed with, "All except for Clancy."

"What are you saying?" Will seemed surprised by Captain Hale's observation.

Thomas went on. "Just look at how Clancy has grown in the weeks she has been with us."

She licked Will's hand. "So?"

Hale walked over to Hubble, who opened a sleepy eye, then closed it again. He patted him on the head. "Will, haven't you noticed that Hubble hasn't grown at all?"

"Do you think he isn't healthy?"

Hale met Will, eye-to-eye. "That's just it! I don't think he is anything at all!" He slipped a small bottle from his coat pocket and took a swig.

"Good God, Thomas – you've completely lost me this time."

Will grabbed the bottle from Hale and threw it overboard. But Hale responded quietly. "Clancy is the only one on this ship who is still alive! The rest of us are in some kind of state of ... of ... *nothing!*"

Will stared at him in disbelief. "You're crazy."

"We must be in between life and death, Will. When we were in that first storm, we didn't make it out alive ... but we didn't die either."

"But what about Clancy?"

"I think that everyone on that schooner experienced a similar fate as we have." He placed his hand on Will's shoulder. "All except for Clancy."

Will was dumbfounded.

"Clancy is still alive! Why just look at her, Will! She's healthy; she eats twice as much as Hubble. She will be twice Hubble's size in no time!" His eyes shifted over to Hubble. "I want Clancy to live."

"So do I."

Just before he opened the door to his quarters, he turned back and said, "It is of great magnitude that we don't waste what time we have."

THOMAS HALE SEQUESTERED himself in his office for the rest of the evening. Nobody had seen him since just after supper, which was very unusual. Will had become concerned so, after the third person asked if anyone had seen Hale, he went to the captain's cabin.

Thomas didn't answer the door right away so when he did, Will pushed past him in the darkness. "Hale, are you alright?"

Hale coughed, rubbed his chest, and then cleared his throat again. With a scratchy voice he said, "As good as I can ever be."

Watching the moonlight through the porthole in the door made patterns on the walls, Will's fingers fumbled for the wall switch before flipping on the light. When his vision had recovered, he was able to see what was on the table in front of him, a collection of photographs, carefully arranged in chronological order, spread out like a timeline.

Thomas looked at him with a despondent expression on his face. "Go away", he said, putting his face in his hands, but not before Will had seen a tear in his eye.

"Hale," Will pleaded, "talk to me." Hale shook his head back and forth. He couldn't talk. Where was his breath?

"I wish I'd never wasted my lifetime sailing these despicable seas."

"If you don't really like this, then why in heaven's name have you spent most of your life out here?"

Hale reached into the pocket of his coat and pulled out a small, crumbling, timeworn, leather journal and handed it to Will.

"What's this?" Will began flipping through it. He looked back at Thomas.

The words became less and less sparse as he read on, the details filling in more and more like a faded memoir.

"These are locations and dates." He continued scanning a few more pages and looked back up. "Places all over the world. This is a record of your voyages throughout your life?"

Hale stared out the window. "Some of it is." He sat back down in the chair, leaning forward. "But most of them are the places I have traveled to, in search of my father." His voice sounded cold and full of resentment, even though the words themselves seemed kindhearted.

Will readjusted so he was sitting up and leaned forward toward Hale. "You haven't mentioned your father before."

"Such a long time ago, really, it feels like an unrelated life."

"What was his name?" Will asked.

Alcohol had always found a way of working into the closed channel of Hale's emotions, allowing his feelings to flow more easily into words. He rested against the chair back and he laughed. "I don't know."

He knew very little about his mother, except that she had been quite the beauty, the daughter of a very wealthy textile merchant in Chicago, and that his father had loved her very much. True love, although they had very limited time to spend together. However, his mother never had the chance to tell his father that she was pregnant. Her parents moved her to Detroit, Michigan and by the time the baby was born, they had insured that she had lost all contact with him.

Thomas, who did not see eye-to-eye with his grandparents from the beginning, asked many times about his father, but was always met with the same answer. Cold silence.

Even after he realized they would never tell him who his father was, Thomas was obsessed with any morsel of information he could find out about him. Where did he come from? What had been his job? Where had he and his mother met? Did he even know he had a son?

Thomas had been sheltered from all of the details of his father; this had left a blank canvas on which he could project any number of fantasies.

Throughout the years, Thomas had overheard the housekeeping staff telling each other rumors about how his mother had been forbidden by her parents from contacting his father, even after she became so gravely ill and begged to see him. They spoke about how her deep sadness brewed storms in the Atlantic, and of her once-gleaming blue eyes, turning the color of ashes after she realized she would never be able to see the love of her life, the father of her three-year-old child, before she died.

The housekeeping staff believed that her unhappiness would make lightning strike, and that her intense misery caused roguish hurricanes to brew, just for her.

"And you mean you have been searching for your father all these years. *That's* the reason you have spent most of your life on the water?"

He nodded. "All I have to go on is that he had aspirations to become a captain on the Great Lakes. It has been my hope that we would surely cross paths sooner or later." Then he closed the log with a snap. He laughed. "And now it's too late. Funny, isn't it?"

"Funny, no. Ironic, yes."

Chapter 32

ON THE SCALE between confusion and frustration, there are many stops. By nightfall, the weather had turned ugly again, with the biting sea bringing a cold drizzle along with it.

She knew the first person she wanted to share the news with was the last person who wanted to hear it – William Stockton. Because, once again, he would be pulled in a different direction.

Will was leaning against the rail when Milly approached him on the deck. She motioned for him to follow her. "Walk with me."

He followed her to her quarters. They shared a few moments of casual conversation, but Milly suddenly stopped and touched Will's shoulder.

"Will, the newspaper changed."

"What?"

"It changed - the date."

"What do you mean the date changed?"

"It's missing."

"I don't follow you. What do you mean *missing*?"

"Gone, Will. It's gone!"

He glanced over at her with a slight arch of the forehead as he lit a new cigarette. His dark eyebrows lifted as if he didn't believe her. She opened the folded paper and handed it to him.

Same paper - *Cleveland Plain Dealer*. But the date was blank - and they watched the print fade in and out, never staying long enough for them to read the print.

She looked warily at Will, gauging his reaction.

Will continued a failed attempt to read the blank pages as the wind picked up outside with the brewing storm. His jaw slowly tightened. He put down the newspaper and stared at her.

How could it be possible?

Will was in shock - suddenly suspicious of her - who she really was, why she really appeared on the *Compass Rose*. He doubted everything she had told him.

He maintained his hostile silence for several long moments. Then, in disbelief, he threw the newspaper at Milly. He swore under his breath. "I don't know why I ever believed you in the first place," he said with an edge of irritation.

His grip on her arm tightened a little and he raised his voice, questioning her. He let out an angry laugh. "You're just a barrel of laughs, aren't you, *fly girl*?"

She hated it when people called her that, and he knew it. "Sarcasm doesn't become you, Will." Milly's tone was judgmental.

"Neither does a lifelong curse." He turned away and then quickly back. He grabbed her firmly by her arm again. "What did you take me for -- a fool?"

"Of course not, Will!" She jerked her arm back and rubbed it. She turned away.

He grabbed her arm and forced her to turn back around. "What the hell?" He shouted, suddenly so defensive that she wasn't sure what to think.

Will shot daggers at her with his eyes. He placed his hands on her shoulders. "Well then how is any of this possible?"

She gave an anguished cry and flung his right hand away with such force that he hit himself in the chest. "I don't know!"

Will, thrown off by her volatility, released her. He stormed off, heading for the pilothouse, leaving her standing alone in her cabin.

The first threatening rumble of thunder seemed the perfect accent to his mood. Menacing clouds began closing in on the *Compass Rose*. The sky darkened and the temperature plummeted. Rain was coming. He could smell it - he could sense the storm dancing on the air.

116

"Fine!" Milly shouted, continuing to stare out the open door at the bruised clouds bobbing above the *Compass Rose*. It looked like thunder and lightning would erupt at any moment.

Fuming, she ran to the door, jerked it shut, and hooked the locking mechanism so it couldn't be opened again. She knew she should go after him and apologize, but she stayed put. He was the one who had started the argument.

Besides, it felt good to yell at somebody.

When she thought of herself, Milly thought of a woman who was smart, capable and practical. She had always prized her toughness under pressure and her ability to go toe-to-toe with an adversary. She was proud to possess that power and strength - rare for a woman in a man's world. Her specific battle arena was one of words, and her display of intelligence and wit had opened many doors for her.

A growing sense of urgency propelled her to open the door again. Just as she stepped onto the deck, the wind slammed into the side of the *Compass Rose*. It felt stronger, wilder than she had ever experienced. The wind blew harder. The gusts of earlier in the evening had succeeded in weakening the structure again, and again, it struck in a frenzy of force. With a terrible tearing growl, the *Compass Rose* began to split

Milly raised her eyes to the furious sky. She cried out Will's name. But there was no sound except a faint, distant rumble, coming closer. Gaining on them.

She screamed again. "*Will! ...!*" But the rising wind snatched her cry of distress and threw it behind her.

Will heard Milly, but when he turned around, he was knocked to the deck by a flying hatch, propelled by the winds. He crawled along the rail, back in the direction her voice had come from.

He inched to his full height, his arms stretched out for balance, leaning into the wind to keep from being carried off. He walked on without glancing back, swallowing the roar in his chest until he couldn't breathe.

The *Compass Rose* rocked, tossed by the burgeoning waves cresting over the sides.

He fought his way onto the bridge and turned on the searchlight, at the risk of being blown overboard. The beam searched the night, in vain.

Will reached Milly on the deck, yanking her back against the door, just as a huge wave engulfed the deck, violently sweeping everything in its way off into the water.

Overhead, the clouds rumbled and the rain thickened. The wind snaked in from the sea and lifted the ends of her hair. Her eyes widened. "You do believe me!"

"No, but I never discount anything!"

The force of the wind snatched the breath from his mouth and made the skin of his face burn. "I'm trying to keep you from …"

She knew Will - and Hale, and Yeager - the others too, thought they were protecting her. But she was not helpless, and she was tired of other people deciding her fate.

She fought him, involuntarily flinging up an arm before her eyes, and then the water struck. She gasped for air and she shouted back at him, letting her rage and determination show.

"I have more courage in *my little finger* than all of you, combined!"

Will watched the ocean writhe beneath the brewing storm. He glanced toward the sky. An army of dark clouds, swollen with rain, was blowing in from the East. He grabbed her arm.

She pushed him away and yelled at him. "I don't need you to keep riding in on your horse to save me!"

Well, get used to it."

Will threw Milly over his shoulder and, raising his voice over the howling wind, he yelled, "Lady, I think you've crossed the line from courageous to stupid!"

He carried her off, warning the crew to stay inside, as they battened down the remaining hatches. They had barely gotten into the pilothouse before a loud crash from outside let them know that they had arrived in the nick of time. His eyes searched the room for the captain.

Then they encountered Captain Hale, at the wheel, but when he spotted Will, he stumbled backward, and he tripped over his own feet, obviously drunk. Then with no warning, he passed out.

Over the course of the voyage, Captain Hale had been able to consume a whole bottle of whiskey in one evening, but he somehow had been able to remain – at least outwardly – sober.

But not that night. Sweat beaded Will's forehead and upper lip as clanking, groaning metal filled the *Compass Rose*, indicating that they were on the move again. They moved slowly at first, then picked up speed, making waves as the water parted in the darkness.

Milly stood, watching the dark water churn underneath the ominous sky, wondering where they were going. Her clothes were soaked with water and perspiration. Her hands felt clammy. She was exhausted. She drew in a deep breath and held it for a moment before letting it whoosh from her lungs. She turned away so he couldn't see the dread in her eyes.

She stared at the distorted image of herself in a tiny mirror on the wheelhouse wall and she wondered if she was dead. Then, in an uncharacteristic attack of panic, she bolted to the door and began pounding it incessantly with her fists, attempting to get out - desperately trying to escape whatever it was that was happening to her.

But Will quickly pulled her back, into a sweaty embrace to calm her. They looked at each other, and the jolt of electricity when her eyes met his had nothing to do with the weather.

The moment was interrupted by a loud, grinding noise. Will glanced over in horror as the wheel began spinning out of control, first clockwise, then counterclockwise.

Will dropped to the floor, at Captain Hale's side and smacked his face several times, to no avail. "Wake up! Get up, you fool!"

Will stepped up to the wheel and reached out to steady it. But before he could reach the brass pedestal, it settled. The *Compass Rose* appeared to be staying its course. Whatever that was. He turned to face Milly and he raised his voice. "Wait here! I will get our engineer to take over!"

But he couldn't move. A flash of fear darkened his face. Will peered down at his hands and realized they were clamped rigidly to the ship's wheel. He noticed his grip was trembling as the wheel took a sharp turn.

The deck slanted suddenly as he involuntarily spun the wheel again, sending anything that was not attached into the railing, causing a string of profanity to spill from his mouth.

Something hit the ship hard, splintering it. Will twisted the wheel, reflexively altering their direction. But rather than finding a grasp he felt himself lose his grip and they began to spin out. He gripped the wheel fiercely and tried to steer through the spin, the terrifying sensation of the water fighting him. Shards of splintered wood were flying through the air and tearing at the flag.

The engines thundered at full throttle, throwing Milly hard, backward against the door. The storm was all around them and he gripped the wheel tighter with each flash and boom.

Through rain as loud as artillery, she watched the storm in alarm, without comment. She took in the roiling water, whitecaps and spray.

Will looked back at Milly, his face masked with worry as he saw the fear in her eyes. She gave him a helpless, frightened look. His face held complete composure and confidence. Milly was certain hers exhibited nothing but terror.

The fury of the wind and rain increased across the night hours as the *Compass Rose* plowed into the roaring sea, thrashing about wildly.

No doubt it had always been one of the most stunning views he had ever seen - the *Atlantic Ocean*. But now it looked anything but beautiful to Will, crashing waves threatening them with ominous menace. Dark clouds billowed overhead, pulsing with electrical energy

Milly choked back a sob, desperately trying to recall the tears forming in the corners of her eyes, but an errant tear escaped and gently slipped down her cheek.

The storm was quickly enveloping them further and he was gripping the wheel tighter with each flash and boom.

"Don't," he said softly, trying to wipe her cheek with his fingers using the one hand he was able to pry loose from the wheel.

The tectonic plates of his heart began to shift. And the *Compass Rose* calmed.

Chapter 33

EVIDENCE. ALL CIRCUMSTANTIAL, but quite convincing. He couldn't positively identify it as such, but he couldn't eliminate it either.

He sat on the edge of the bed in the small, cluttered cabin with his chin in his hands, deep in thought.

Captain Hale walked in. "What are you reading?" he asked.

Will held up the newspaper with the front page facing Hale.

Hale took a deep breath and blew out. "Will, I cannot understand how you jumped so quickly from not believing in anything to frolicking around with ghosts ..." he looked back at Will and gestured toward his face. "... wearing spectacles that don't belong to you."

Will slowly removed the glasses and placed them in his pocket.

Hale went on. "Where did you get those, anyway? ... From the apparitions on that ship?"

Will handed the newspaper to Hale again. "Read the paper, Hale."

He took the paper from him. "So?" He turned it over without opening it. "*The Cleveland Plain Dealer*. Nothing very remarkable about that." He handed it back to Will and turned to leave.

"... from ...... 1937?" Will asked.

Hale stopped. He turned back around. "What did you say?" He jumped back, sweeping the paper from Will's hands. And he began to read.

"Brace yourself," Will said. "The ride is about to begin."

"Hale slowly handed the paper back to Will and said, "And that's not the half of it. It's not from 1937, Will. Take a closer look."

Will opened the paper and his heart almost stopped.

August 23, 1950. But the day of the month and the rest of the paper was blank. Will felt the world spinning around him as he tried to process the typed date in front of him.

Why had it previously been 1937 and now 1950? Was there some significance of those particular years?

There was only one person on board who might have clues that might help him find the answers to the new barrage of questions forming in his head. It was time for another visit with their resident fly girl.

THAT AFTERNOON, HE went to find her, but he was distracted by the sound of voices and laughter wafting up from below. Milly was in the galley, answering historical questions about happenings since 1926, many of which were being met with dismay and varying degrees of skepticism.

When Will finally caught up with her again, she was leaving the galley. She stopped when she saw him observing her from across the deck.

He walked slowly toward her and stopped when they were only a heartbeat apart. "Truce?"

Milly smiled. "The jury is still out. But I might cut you a little slack."

They walked together, at first with no conversation between them, but the elephant in the room soon became too difficult to ignore. Will stopped and turned her to face him. "I thought the newspaper headline was a story about the plane that was going around the world in 1937."

She nodded her head. "That's what I told you. Did you forget?"

He raised his hand, "Just hold on a minute. You don't know the most recent chapter in this story yet."

Will stared down at the headline on the front page of the *Plain Dealer* and whistled low and long.

"Not exactly 1937," he said, passing her the newspaper to read. "It looks like this paper is from the year 1950."

She shuddered. "How frightening to catch a glimpse of the future."

Will laughed. "Well, it didn't seem to bother you when you showed it to me when it was from 1937 -- that's the future for me, you know."

His eyes crinkled around the edges. "Let's just see what we find." He pulled out a deck chair and gestured for her to return the paper to him.

Will opened the newspaper. "August …," he paused and gave a little huff – the day was blurred, "1950."

Usual depressing stuff. He didn't even know why he ever picked up the paper to read it. Then he realized the reason why it was so important. Because it might be more dangerous to ignore the news than to have to learn about it. Ignorance could be deadly. Especially in their case.

Will scoured the *Plain Dealer*, absorbing as much information and history as he could. Maybe it would be - - - He dropped the paper.

Dear God. He was staring down at the face on the society page of the newspaper. His brother's face.

Captain John Stockton.

Stop shaking and read the story. He quickly scanned the article, then pushed the newspaper away, as if it was making him ill. Milly picked it up.

"John Stockton? Your brother?"

Will hastily swept the newspaper from Milly and looked at it again.

The article in the 1950 Cleveland paper, as Will began to read it, outlined the generous financial assistance many local charities had recently received, thanks to a windfall that year, from the *Stockton Foundation*. It made him smile.

But his smile quickly faded as he read on. Beads of sweat formed along his collar. His heart sped up.

There were two additional stories about the history of the *Stockton Foundation*.

His eyes settled on an article outlining the history of the foundation. He smiled at the old photograph of a beaming John Stockton in a tuxedo and tie at a party. Katie stood beside him, wearing the sapphire party dress she had loved so dearly, as beautiful as ever. Next to Katie stood two women, one of them much older than the other, both dripping in jewels.

He let out a snort. "Abigail and Phoebe Simpson." His eyes slid over the article, skimming through what he already knew, but he stopped when he got to the part with the sad story of John and Katie Stockton. He nodded in agreement that Katie had left this world far too soon. His eyes jumped to the next line.

Will fell back onto the seat as he began deciphering the biography about John.

John Stockton was one of the most successful businessmen of his time. **Was?**

Wait! He held the paper closer to his face. *John?*

"What?" Will shouted from behind the sheets of paper in his hands.

That's impossible! He can't be dead! Why, I just saw him as we left the Port of Cleveland - not that long ago! ... Or was it? He turned away, stunned by what he had just read.

John had died. He still couldn't believe it. He had just seen him a few months ago.

When he got to the part about John's mysterious disappearance and presumed drowning in 1926, a tear escaped from the corner of his eye. He shut them both as tight as he could, hoping that somehow, when he opened them again, the newspaper would be back on the year 1937 ... better yet - 1926.

Will's heart sank. His hands were trembling so badly that he had to put the newspaper down.

How could John be dead?

Will wasn't naive enough to believe that his brother had simply ended his own life. He needed to speak with him. But of course, it was too late.

He picked up the paper again. There was a benefit being held in a month, by a Mrs. Abigail Simpson, to support the cause. *Hah! Abigail Simpson! There she is again!*

He scanned down the page further and stopped at another article written about the life of Captain John Stockton. He got very quiet.

"What is it, Will?" Milly touched his shoulder.

But he didn't hear a word she said. His eyes were glued to the story he was reading in the *Plain Dealer*, dated August *something*, 1950. The words surprised him. They hardly seemed conclusive.

Will brushed a finger over the page, his gaze wistful and far away. His face blazed in sudden rage. He swiveled away from Milly, dropped the paper, face-up, on the table, and extended his hands, palms out, toward her.

Before them, spread out, across a full page of the *Plain Dealer*, was the sad, mysterious story of the lost crew aboard a ship, owned by Captain John Stockton, that had sailed through a crack in the Atlantic Ocean, taking all hands along with it.

He combed through the obituaries of those aboard the *Compass Rose*. The details were great, enough to paint a complete portrait of each of the twelve men who had shared the ship.

"Holy crap!"

Under normal circumstances, Will had considered research a form of relaxing recreation. But this time he wasn't doing it for recreation. It was more like doing it for his own survival.

After quickly scanning the story again, he folded the newspaper and placed it on the chair beside him.

She had made the conscious decision not to reveal her true identity in the beginning. But that was before she knew that the ship she was on had met its demise long before she had become a global sensation. It was time to come clean.

Chapter 34

*"THAT NEWSPAPER STORY from 1937 was about **you?**"* Will ran his hands through his hair. *"You're* Amelia Earhart?"

She nodded, in silence.

Will recalled reading about a young woman who had set the women's altitude record of 14,000 feet in the early nineteen twenties, but he hadn't been convinced that a woman had actually accomplished such a feat.

Milly tried to find a reference point that might make it easier for Will to relate to. But as she explained that she replicated the success of the first solo, non-stop flight across the Atlantic Ocean by Charles Lindbergh, in 1928, she realized that Will would have no recollection of Lindbergh's feat, much less that of her own.

"Where's your plane? And didn't you have a raft on your plane with you?" He asked with some skepticism.

Amelia tried to explain what she remembered, but much of it wasn't clear.

"I tried to drag the raft ashore, but it tore on the rocks. So I tied the pieces of the raft on the trees as markers. For Itasca."

"Who's Itasca?"

"The Itasca is a ship." She explained further. "I had radio contact with them." She closed her eyes again. "They were helping me. They were my only hope."

"My navigator was gone." She rubbed her temples. "It's all so cloudy."

Her voice trembled. "I was sure somebody would find me – my plane was easy to spot, sitting out in the reef."

"But on the next day, the tide rolled in the action of the waves and flipped the Electra. It was completely covered in water. All of it."

"Nobody came searching for you?"

"Yes, there was one that I knew about."

"Wait a minute. I'm getting confused."

"I was on the opposite side of the island, scouting for food and water."

"But if you left yellow scraps tied to the trees …"

She slid into a sitting position and leaned against one of the open hatch doors. "The search plane must have identified my markers. I saw them zooming the markers, but they never spotted me." She flinched as she struggled to sit up straight. "At least, I don't think they saw me. I screamed and I waved, but they were looking in the wrong place."

Will continued to probe. "But they must have seen some sign of the plane, in the water."

"Shortly after the Electra was overturned in the water, I went back to see if I could get to it and gather some of my things before it was pulled out further into the sea." She wrung her hands. "But when I got there, the Electra was gone."

Will placed his hand on hers and gave her an empathic look.

"After a few days … or was it weeks …" she said, with a lost expression on her face, "I came to the conclusion that if I was to have even a slim chance of survival that I would have to get off that island."

All she knew for sure was that she wasn't sure about anything. After existing for days on end, she was able to drift on the ocean floating on a makeshift raft, until that night she spotted the *Compass Rose*.

"Why didn't you tell me about all of this before?"

Milly smiled broadly and adjusted her hat with an unsteady hand. "If I had told you right off, would you have believed me?"

He narrowed his eyes at Milly. "You're a sneak." He smiled.

"Maybe so. But now that we know each other so well, we shouldn't be afraid to tell the truth."

Will motioned for her to follow him.

She gazed at him in bewilderment. "What are you doing?"

"I'm doing the only thing I can do. Pull up a chair. I think I have a lot of it figured out already."

He showed her the paper full of notes, crossed out sentences and questions. "Though there are a few things that don't make sense."

Will's eyes shone under brows gathered in concern. "Talk to me." His expression was grim. "Tell me everything. Should I be worried?" He paused. "Do you know anything about what happened to the *Compass Rose*, eleven years before your trip around the world?"

Milly touched his sleeve. "I've told you everything I know."

She gave him a whimsical look. "Well I didn't exactly make it around the world, did I?" She sighed, lost in thought. "I wonder now if it was worth the risk I took."

"Failure is a necessary part of the journey," he added. "Look at it like this. If you hadn't taken that risk, we would never have met."

She hugged him. Her eyes went upward as a lone tern circled above them, high in the sky. She sighed. "What I wouldn't give for another chance to take the Electra up ... and finish that trip."

Will smiled at her and touched her shoulder. "Milly, I wish I knew how to make that possible for you."

She returned the smile and took in a deep breath and she exhaled slowly. "For now, I will just have to settle for a nice supper."

ON THEIR WAY back to her quarters after their meal, Milly walked alongside Will while they continued to compare their lives, laughing at the many differences and marveling at the many more similarities. She rested just around the turn from her cabin and stared out into the water.

He stood next to her. It was too black to see the sea below. There had been no visible stars that night. Will imagined himself, using the stars alone for guidance. How many people missed him and his talks on the constellations he gave at the observatory?

Will combed the sky, straining his eyes for a tiny, passing glimpse of a star. He longed for that sense of accomplishment when someone had finally grasped the art of gauging the stars for direction. He squinted into the heavens, searching for just one little star, and he wondered for a brief moment … if there was an approach, using the constellations to find their way to a particular island, even though they had no idea where they were.

He regained his common sense and smiled weakly. He tilted his head back to the main deck of the *Compass Rose*. But within a few seconds, his head snapped back up and he stared skyward. Out-of-the-blue, there appeared streaks of light in the night sky. Will abruptly leaped onto the ladder and began climbing, Milly on his tail. When he reached the upper deck, he ran to the rail. His heart stopped. Panting, he pointed to another blip in the cool night sky.

These were no ordinary stars. They were movements of heavenly bodies. … *shooting stars!* The wheels in his head began turning.

Milly, attempting to catch her breath, asked, "What's wrong, Will?"

No sooner had she gotten the words out of her mouth, when another one followed. Her eyes grew wide. She gasped at the trailing sparkles of warmth. "How beautiful!"

Will faced Milly. "Those were shooting stars! And there were three of them!"

"I'm afraid I don't know very much about them, other than they are beautiful."

"Shooting stars have always reminded me that we are connected to the universe," said Will.

Milly smiled. "I have only seen one before, when I was a little girl. My father used to say that if you saw one, it meant that you will achieve your destiny."

Will gave her a doubtful look.

She caught the expression on his face and explained further. "Not the physical one, but the spiritual one." She touched his arm. "You know, Will, you are supposed to make a wish when you see one. And it is said that whatever you wish for will eventually come true."

He thought about how much he would have loved to have made a wish for Milly - a wish that somehow he could find a way to help her get back to the Electra. He threw up his hands and laughed out loud. "Of course. And naturally, we both missed our opportunity … *three times!"*

At that very moment, something caught the corner of Will's eye. As if on cue, a bluish ball appeared, just like a rocket with a white streaking trail behind it. It lasted for only a few seconds, but there was no doubt in either of their minds. It was number four.

He glanced over at Milly, but she was staring up into the heavens. Then, with the hope that it wasn't too late, he did his best impression of a man, making a wish.

WILL'S BRAIN WAS running a million miles an hour with ideas as he lay in bed that night. Sleep was impossible. He jumped out of his bed and sat at the table, writing, drawing … scribbling.

After three hours, he stared down at the paper in front of him. All at once, it came to him. He jumped up, tripping and struggling to pull his trousers and shirt back over his undergarments.

Could he do it? Could he use the stars to help locate the island Milly had told them about? Would they find her plane there? Was it even possible? Who knew? But it was certainly worth a shot.

Chapter 35

"ARE YOU GOING to tell me what this is all about?" she asked quietly. "You disappeared right after we saw the shooting stars, without explanation, and now you tumble me out of my bed in the middle of the night and whisk me out here with the briefest explanation possible."

He grimaced. "I'm sorry. But I have been working on an idea." He took three steps away and then spun back around with a grin. "Let's find your island!"

"William Stockton," Milly shouted back at him, in a whisper, to keep the rest of them from hearing. "You're crazy!"

There was a light in his eyes that illuminated the night sky. He led her to the chart room, next to the pilothouse.

Will pulled out a piece of paper he had hidden in his jacket and spread it out on top of a cabinet. He smiled back at her.

"You're not easy to read." She frowned and stared at him. He stared right back at her. Then he made funny face.

She tried not to laugh and it came out like a snort, which made them both laugh even harder.

"I don't know how to say it."

"Just tell me."

Will took Milly by the elbow and guided her to the cabinet. "There." He pointed down to the paper.

It was a map. Of the seas.

Cartography wasn't his strong point. Still, he had watched his brother John redraw maps from maritime reports, setting out new information in relation to what was already known. What mattered was having reference points that put the new information into proper perspective.

Will had drawn in constellations and stars, with numbers next to them. There were arrows and lines leading in every direction. Milly's eyes blurred as she struggled to make some sense of his map.

He thought for a moment and then picked up the pencil lying beside the blotter. He began to draw in the *Compass Rose*.

"But we don't have any reference points, Will. This is impossible."

Will smiled a little crooked smile and, in a very calm voice, he said, "Wait ..."

"I don't see anything, Will!" She strained her eyes, impatiently waiting for some kind of clarification.

"Watch very closely." He pointed again, to the crudely drawn map.

She blew a stray curl out of her eye with a hasty puff of air.

Will had sketched the *Compass Rose* at the far end of the paper, far away from the rest of the objects on the map.

Milly was exasperated. It took a few seconds to see it, but the ship, the little sketch Will had drawn of the *Compass Rose*, was moving. On its own.

Time stilled, her breath caught in her throat. Will's eagerness infected her spirit, filling it with a buoyancy she had not felt in months. Her eyes followed the vessel as it moved toward the stars he had drawn at the top of the paper.

"This isn't a map." Milly gasped." It's a prophecy."

Will gazed at her face. She was right; it was much more than a map.

"It's amazing, Will," Milly whispered. "How did you do it?"

"I have no idea," Will answered candidly. "I just outlined what I saw in my mind's eye. But when I went back to it later, it seemed very different than what I had first envisioned.

Milly's eyes grew as big as saucers. "What does it mean?"

Will beamed at his own brilliance. "I'm not sure. But it has to be some kind of sign."

Chapter 36

LIGHT FROM THE rising sun flooded the room, painting the countertops and utensils with a golden glow.

Yeager loved the way his kitchen looked in the morning, before anything was touched, the utensils gleaming over the metal countertop, the glassware and baking pans lined up in the cabinets.

It always seemed to be just waiting for him. He stopped and took it all in, his senses feeling not with his memories but with the feeling of possibility.

Milly came from behind surprising him by touching his shoulder. He turned and faced her.

Yeager had to be at least sixty years of age. Deep lines coursed through his leathery, tanned face, but her gaze was drawn to his eyes, blue and bright as an autumn sky.

He asked her, "What's the best thing you'd like for breakfast?"

"Blueberry muffins," she said without hesitation.

"Well," Yeager replied, picking up his book of recipes. "We've never had blueberries, but I think I can come up with something very close." He fired up the gas oven.

Most of the ingredients and utensils were stored where they had always been - in the big pantry. Milly followed Yeager into the storeroom. She took in a deep breath.

"What are you doing?" he asked her.

"It has the scent of flour and spices."

The iron Griswold muffin pan was in the baking drawer. Yeager would never use any cast iron but Griswold. He pointed to the book in front of her. "You read."

She sat on a bar stool at the cook's counter, and they got to work.

Milly narrated the recipe to Yeager as they put together the ingredients - eggs and milk, a dab of melted butter and the dry ingredients.

Yeager's kitchen felt like a separate ship. It overlooked the portside deck, and enveloped Milly in its warmth, with understated simplicity and jars of spices lining the ledge beneath the window.

"This is fun," she said. She smiled at him. "I love baking from scratch with my friends. Do you have many friends, Yeager?"

Ignoring the question, Yeager said, "I think we need a little more milk." As he walked to the refrigerator, Milly followed behind, continuing their conversation. Yeager stopped talking to her when he opened the refrigerator door.

"I thought you said we didn't have any blueberries, Yeager," she said.

"We don't," he replied.

But there it was - a two-quart container - a wooden basket filled to the brim with fresh blueberries. Not just any blueberries - big, luscious, fat, juicy blueberries.

He was dumbfounded. And for that matter, so was Milly.

Yeager wiped his sticky hands on his apron and he sat next to Milly on a stool at the counter.

She was deep in thought. "Yeager –" Milly's gaze narrowed on him. "Do you know who I am? I mean, who I *really* am?"

He spoke without looking in her direction. "I have never been good at remembering faces unless I see them regularly," he reflected as he measured the flour into a cup and placed it in the mixing bowl.

She apologized for trying to take over in his kitchen earlier. "I'm sorry if I hurt you, Yeager."

"I'm not hurt. In fact, it's just the opposite. Being in this kitchen makes me very happy now. You helped me learn to be grateful for what I have and you made me see that there is always a way to make something good with it!"

"Tell me, Milly - What was it about flying that drew you to it?

136

"I guess I think what drew me to it was the sense of freedom …" Her mind drifted back to her earliest memories of flying. She smiled, whimsically. "… and discovery."

"Actually, my first "flight" was when I was seven years old. With the help of my sister and my uncle, I made a wooden roller coaster."

Yeager squinted his eyes at her. "What does that have to do with any of this?"

She laughed and he saw the little girl she must have been at that age.

Then she went on. "After a spectacular crash, I told my sister that it was just like flying."

"And years later, I went to visit my sister in Toronto, Canada. And one day, at an aviation expo, a pilot flew his plane very close to me."

Yeager stiffened and his eyes widened. "That must have scared you!"

But Milly shook her head and grinned. "I believed that little red airplane said something to me as it swished by."

They discussed Milly's life, but she spoke only about her life as Milly, and not of *the famous Amelia Earhart*. She told Yeager about her life as a young girl, growing up in Atchison, Kansas, at the turn of the century.

"Good fortune seems to have followed you throughout your whole life."

She pulled her mind back to the present with that comment. Memory lane was a lovely place to visit, but she lived in the real world - or some facsimile of it. Her hand tightened on the cup as she saw the expression in Yeager's eyes.

"I may have said too much already, Milly. I only meant that you were lucky."

They chatted about the *Compass Rose* and her rich history, intertwined with the legacy of the Stockton family. They talked about Yeager and his life before he was a cook, his hopes and the dreams he had for his life, as captain of a ship like the *Compass Rose*.

Before he knew it, he had touched on a topic he hadn't intended on telling anybody. Ever. Milly listened with interest, concern and misty-eyed empathy as he ended the tale.

"And I missed those years while my son was growing up … all because I didn't even know I had a son."

Milly touched his arm. "Does your son know who you are now?"

"No."

"Yeager. You must find him and explain to him …" She stopped. There was no point in finishing the sentence. He could never tell him now.

Yeager turned away from Milly and he said, "Even if it was possible to tell him now, it's too late. I'm sure he would hate me. And there would be nothing to talk about." He rubbed his neck. "That would be like two adults, trying to start from scratch."

Milly asked, "Like you and me?" She leaned in and gave him a nudge. "We don't know much about each other, but I would like to be your friend."

"I would like that too."

"Well, then I guess we'll just have to *start from scratch,* Yeager. Won't we?"

Yeager said nothing. And then he smiled.

Milly read more from the cookbook. "Milk, sugar, butter - and a touch of maple." The slowly melded blend brought a smile to her face.

While the muffins baked, he made another pot of coffee and set up cream and sugar, butter and jam. The smell of the baking muffins filled the kitchen.

A lump pressed against Yeager's throat and he wiped his eyes with the back of his hand. He apologized. "I am just an old fool."

She stood and wiped her hands on the apron. "There is absolutely nothing wrong with showing emotion."

He gave her a puzzled look and asked her, "How can you say that it's *good to be sad?*"

Milly replied. "Oh Yeager - think about it!" She plopped down on the stool and spun around to face him.

Yeager was puzzled.

She smiled. "It's good to let sadness out. Because that makes more room for joy!"

Chapter 37

CLEVELAND MIGHT JUST as well have been in another galaxy.

Early stars began to appear as the bluish-gray haze settled in. Will draped himself in his sad memory of John, because it was the closest thing to having him around.

Sitting in a deck chair, he stretched his legs out in front of him and leaned back to search the stars. Behind him, tiny distant lights from the futuristic city of Cleveland raised a faint golden glow where the water met the sky.

No doubt, the city would be on their agenda, but apparently not yet.

It had appeared shortly after they sailed out of the last storm. But whenever the *Compass Rose* attempted to navigate closer to the Cleveland shore, they were met with a seemingly invisible wall. A radiant, golden world waited on the other side - - enticing, unreachable. They could see it – almost taste it. But that was all. So, for now, they had to be satisfied to hold onto it as a beautiful backdrop to whatever was in store for them.

Milly had sensed Will struggling emotionally, after reading the newspaper articles about John, realizing so much time had passed, so when she saw him on the deck, she dropped down and sat on a chair next to him.

"Is this seat taken?"

He sat motionless, in silence.

She tried again. "Penny for your thoughts."

After a minute or two, Will spoke in a voice void of emotion. "The sunset. Drink it in. Appreciate it. It's the most beautiful sight this side of purgatory."

She touched his arm.

He analyzed her face. "My brother, John, was my best friend, and I never got the chance to say goodbye." He inhaled deeply, and then he exhaled. "It really doesn't matter, Milly, does it?"

She smiled. "Of course it matters, Will!" She patted his arm. "Once you have a brother, you don't stop having him just because you can no longer see or touch him." Milly hugged her knees to her chest and sighed.

"Goodbyes can be painful, can't they? Yet, when we don't get a chance to say them, we can be hurt even more."

It was her turn to study his face. "There must have been a dozen women back home, vying for your attention, Will."

"Well," he said, unable to keep himself from smiling. "I'm flattered." He went on. "So, you think I'm handsome?"

Milly skewered him with a razor sharp glare. She huddled against the wall to keep out of the wind. "Yes, until you open your mouth and your remarkable ego slips out. Then the effect is spoiled."

Even shivering against the wall with her lips tinged blue, she looked delightful as she peeked up at him. He loved that she never let anybody push her around.

Arms folded across her chest, she probed. "Did you have a good relationship with your family - your parents?"

"I have no interest in dredging up the past."

"What about your wife?"

He faced her. "If you must know - yes, I have scars from my past."

Milly said, "We all have them. Scars are just another kind of memory, Will."

"No wife." He pulled a cigarette from his jacket and put it to his lips. He motioned, offering one to Milly, but she shook her head.

"Well, whoever she was, she must have broken your heart for it to be so painful to talk about."

"Actually, I was the one who ended it." He turned away from her.

"I told you about my failed attempt to fly around the world, even though it is a horrible memory for me. The least you could do is reciprocate."

Will glanced to the deck just below them, to the voices coming from the galley.

"They can't hear us," she said. "Talk. Unless you're afraid, of course."

After a few moments of silence, Milly apologized. "You don't have to tell me about it. It's none of my business."

But William Stockton accepted the challenge. He pulled his chair a little closer to hers and lowered his voice.

"Her name was Maggie." And he went on, not able to hold back any longer. "She was the most beautiful woman I have ever known. She had the face of an angel. But also the mind of an eagle."

"So, what happened?" Milly asked him.

Will didn't answer the question.

"Might I ask you a pointed question, Will?" Milly looked up and met his eyes. "Was there an affection between you and Maggie?"

"Affection was the reason we drifted apart."

Milly sat up straight and cocked her head slightly to one side, in question. "Will, that doesn't make any sense."

Images of that long ago night roared in. Will allowed himself to slip back in time...

The room was crowded. He had been working late at the observatory when he'd realized he was supposed to be at the annual board of directors dinner, giving a speech.

Will was obviously disheveled when he arrived at the venue. As he desperately attempted to tidy up his appearance, in secret before his talk, he was startled by a voice coming from behind him.

"William Stockton..."

He turned and was met with the smile of one of his students from the observatory - a young seamstress with aspirations to be an astronomer - Maggie. Only she was different than she had ever been during his class. She was beautiful, but in a sweet, innocent way. For the first time in his life, he couldn't think of anything intelligent to say.

With Maggie's assistance and quick thinking, William Stockton was able to walk out onto the stage as if he had spent hours primping and preparing for his oration, impressing the crowd so much with his confidence that he was offered a highly sought–after fellowship.

The two quickly became inseparable.

He saw his cigarette glowing in the dark, the ash dangling for a moment before disappearing into the water.

Will closed his eyes again and he smiled. He felt all warm inside.

"It sounds to me like you were very happy, Will. What happened?" Milly asked quietly, although she sensed that the pleasant memory was most likely skating on thin ice.

Will's face slowly crumpled. As the memory continued, it took a painful twist. "We quarreled and then I ended it." He tossed the cigarette over the side.

"Just like that? What could you have been arguing over that was so bad that you would end everything?"

He glanced away from her and said nothing.

"Will." Milly touched his arm again. "Maybe if you talk about it, you will feel better."

He faced her. After a long pause, he told her what had haunted him for years. "I am a man. I have needs."

Milly eyed him, connecting the dots. "Oh."

"Maggie was my one true love." He gazed back out onto the lake again. He took in a deep breath. "I suppose you could say I needed more than she wanted to give me … at the time."

He pulled another cigarette from his jacket pocket, placed it between his lips, but then suddenly he ripped it back out, propelling it over the rail. "When she told me that she was not ready, I should have understood. But I didn't. We quarreled."

"I told her that if she wasn't ready then, I didn't wish to continue the relationship." His shoulders drooped. "I can still see the expression on her face."

Milly's heart did a series of flips as he told her the rest of the story.

"A few weeks before my brother's wedding, she drowned while on a long vacation with her family."

Milly sat quietly and smiled weakly at him. "Oh Will. I am so sorry."

"I was insanely jealous, you know. I wanted her back the moment I ended the relationship."

142

Her eyes shifted back to his. "But not enough to follow her?"

"I loved Maggie. I was planning to ask her to marry me when she returned."

"Did you write to her? Did you at least give her some indication of what was going on?"

"I wanted to. I did, in fact, write to her. Dozens of letters."

"She never answered them?"

"I never mailed them. I'm not very good at expressing myself, Milly."

"Everything I wrote sounded so hollow. I had to see her face to face. I had to be able to look into her eyes and see for myself whether she would ever be able to love me again."

She stared at him, open-mouthed. "Will … What were you thinking, keeping all of that to yourself?"

"I suppose I wanted to ride in on my horse and save the day." He looked down and added. "But I was too late."

"That's so sad, Will. How did you go on?"

"In time, the grief turned into a dull ache with occasional flares of agony. It was like a fading bruise." He took in a deep breath and let it out. "I forgot about it until I bumped into a memory. It was the little moments that pierced most sharply - the remembrance of her smile, a gesture, a soft voiced phrase."

"I will never know what would have been, had things played out differently for us … if we hadn't quarreled, and if she hadn't gone away with her family and been in that horrible accident."

Will studied Milly's face. Part of him felt betrayed to think that anybody else was privy to one of the most intensely personal, intensely private, and utterly shameful moments of his life. The other part felt an immense relief that it really wasn't some deep, dark secret only he bore, and bore alone. Anymore.

There were other memories, though, that he had been careful not to share, like the time when...

Will shoved himself back to the present, not wanting to recollect any more of his mistakes. At least, not for now. He cleared his throat and Milly realized he hadn't meant to say that much. Her cheeks warmed. She pushed the hair out of her eyes.

Will stared at her, seized by the feeling that maybe she didn't really exist. Maybe none of them did. "It's been hell, quite honestly." He fell silent.

Milly looked into his eyes and found an openness there, an expression of compassion and concern that shook her to the core. It had an immediate effect on her.

The light gale wind whispered and a feathery rain misted over them. In the distance, thunder rolled in tympanic majesty, a rhythmic backbeat to the sensations growing in their bodies.

She leaned into him, her hands on his forearms. Somehow, his hands wound up on her hips. Her lips brushed his cheek. If he turned his head an inch ....

They could fight it no longer. So they kissed.

... with all the passion of tepid tea.

It just didn't feel right. They pulled back slowly and looked at each other, with peculiar expressions. Will sat down hard in a deck chair.

Milly giggled. "That was like kissing my brother."

Will feigned shock. She threw a crumpled up ball of paper at him - he caught it and pitched it back to her. She elbowed him hard and he pretended to fall off the chair.

Milly appreciated his sensitivity, not to demand more of her. He was too wise for that, she thought. She loved that about him. She had such strong feelings for him, and she knew he felt the same. Maybe this just wasn't the right time.

While lost in thought, Will had been absently rubbing a knot on the back of his neck. She noticed.

He turned the full force of his twinkle on Milly. "Well, you didn't exactly put much feeling into it either."

"Will, what's wrong with your neck?" She examined him, running her hand down the right side, stopping at a knot, just under the skin's surface. "How long have you had this?" She began to knead her fingers into the swelling.

He shrugged. "Since the last time I had a good nights' sleep. Frankly, I cannot remember the time when it hasn't been there."

Milly examined his face. "You've got dark circles under your eyes. Didn't you get any sleep at all last night?"

He didn't say anything.

"Tension. You need to learn to relax," she continued as she worked the muscle a little bit harder.

He winced. She paused and made a motion with her hand toward the deck. "Up."

Will gave her a look of confusion. "Up?"

144

She grinned. "Yes. Your place or mine?"

Will's heart begin to pound. *Was that an innuendo?* She flustered him a bit, but he didn't want her to notice.

Milly stood and waited for him to stand. "If I am going to give your neck a proper rubdown, we need to find a more conducive place than on a drafty deck of this ship."

Will led the way, and they left the moon, the stars and the sea behind.

Sometimes the full moon provided enough light to navigate to his quarters, but not this evening; the moon was the shape of a wood shaving. He bumped into Milly as he reached for the handle to the door. Without meaning to, she brushed his left hand as he slid open the door and stepped down two steps into the cabin.

The left wall of the room contained different shelves with glass doors and locks, and beyond that sat a small bed. Against the far wall stood a large desk next to a small sofa.

He retreated to the couch and braced himself on the armrest as Milly's voice continued. "I don't know why you are so jumpy, Will. It's not as if I am planning to take advantage of you in your weakened state." She looked over at him again, as she watched him still trying to balance himself on the edge of the lumpy sofa. Despite his obvious consternation, she couldn't help but giggle.

"Milly, it's just a pain in my neck."

"… and Will, before you say it -- don't." Milly gave him a wink. "I will continue to be a *pain in the neck* until I am confident you will take proper care of yourself."

Milly sat on the sofa and turned slightly in his direction.

He rubbed his thumbs over his eyelids and said, "I will be just fine after I get some rest."

"Let me be the judge of that." She patted the spot next to her on the sofa. "Now, get down here."

He grinned as he slid off the armrest. And she went to work.

AN HOUR LATER, Milly grinned down at the man whose head was resting comfortably in her lap. "Just relax … and sleep."

"Yes ma'am." His eyes were closing. "I'm in your hands…"

For the moment, he was in her hands. Tomorrow or the next day, it might be different. But she would take tonight and hold it close.

Sometime before dawn, Milly opened her eyes and found Will standing in front of the porthole, watching in silence.

To him it was a different place than from just hours ago. He wasn't sure if he should say what was on his mind, so he just smiled. "Care to join me? Sometimes I like to watch the brightness seep into the world, like spun glass."

Milly's indecision lasted barely a second as she slipped her hand in his.

Just after daybreak, he quietly walked her to the door of her quarters, and as he started back down the deck, she called after him. He looked back over his shoulder. Milly was smiling softly, and he smiled back.

It lifted the weight of grief from his past and chased the shadows from his heart. Restoration was on the horizon...

And healing was on its way.

Chapter 38

THUNDER RUMBLED, AND lightning lit up the dark sky. The sound grew from a few taps to a roar.

Rain suddenly poured from the heavens, as if it had been turned on by an enormous spigot. The thunder boomed again, only louder this time.

Hale throttled up in the wheelhouse and Milly stood on the deck watching, while the anchor chains squealed back into their casing, Another giant shadow faded into the obscurity of the dark sky.

A few moments of quiet followed, but not for long. The wind strengthened again, and with it came another torrential downpour.

They were on their way again.

When Will caught up with Milly, it was during a lull in the action, and she had left her quarters for a breath of air. It was obvious she was feeling doubtful. Doubtful that they would locate the island. Doubtful that they would find the Electra. Doubtful that she would ever fly again.

Will sighed inwardly, found his signature smile, and swiveled to face her. "Don't worry, Milly. I am confident that we will find the island."

She gave him a grateful smile, but when she searched his face, his expression reflected nothing but abrupt bafflement.

He seized her arm tightly and jerked her backward, hard against the galley door. She hit her head as the ship leaned hard to portside, immediately followed by a tilt in the opposite direction.

Mountains of steel-gray lake water, with long streamers of spray and foam flowing from their peaks, ghostly emerged in the half-light through the clouds overhead.

Milly slipped and slid down the steep starboard list of *the Compass Rose* like a skier down a mountainside, faster and faster, toward her cabin.

Will shouted orders to her. "It would be best if you stayed in your cabin until this clears up, Milly!"

There were many sarcastic things she could have said back to him, and she would have, if she hadn't been fighting so hard to prevent herself from taking an impromptu evening swim.

The high-pitched whine of the rigging morphed into a deeper note as the walls of water continued to pummel the ship. She managed to grasp the door handle to her cabin and dive inside before the door slammed shut behind her.

Back in his own quarters, Will sat at the desk and stared at the radio - on, but not much company, because it was dead.

Another brush with irony. He smiled.

Chapter 39

CAPTAIN HALE POSSESSED eyes so blue they were almost transparent. There was a vaporous, ethereal quality about him. He reveled in these post-storm mornings when the air smelled moist and felt fresh and renewed.

Especially when he knew they were once again on the ocean. It was in the atmosphere.

He traced the route on Will's map with his finger - the one next to the missing digit. "We will ...," he said, with a faintly amused expression, as though laughing at some private but good-natured joke, "... go on this wild goose chase."

"I believe we will be able to go ashore, for a short burst of time, as long as we are mindful of our distance from the *Compass Rose* and the particular time of day." Will was optimistic, remembering the entry in the log that outlined their allowances and limits.

"If we locate the island," Hale continued.

Will interrupted. "... **When** we find the island."

Hale rolled his eyes and boomed, finishing his sentence. "The men will go ashore - and only the men!"

Milly jumped up. "I'm going too!"

Hale barely glanced in her direction. "No place for a woman. I forbid it! Susie stays here!"

Milly's face fell. She stood. "You can't forbid *me* from going. *It's my plane!*" She took a small step back, and for a moment Hale thought she was going to crumble.

He was wrong. She caught herself and straightened.

"I want to go."

"I'm afraid I can't allow you to do that," Hale said. "It's settled." And he started for his cabin.

Milly's mouth worked as she struggled to maintain her composure. Her temper ratcheted higher. She clenched her teeth together to keep herself from saying something she would regret.

She felt a hand, from behind, squeeze her left shoulder. Yeager stepped forward. His wrinkly face suddenly went pale, making his eyes seem bluer than ever, and then it happened. His chuckle filled the deck and made Milly smile, despite her disappointment. She was beginning to realize how much she had misjudged him in the beginning.

"Thomas …" he approached Captain Hale, "… I think it would be a mistake to forbid her to go." He smiled over at Milly. It was as if they had turned another corner. Yeager followed the captain to his quarters.

MEN! ARROGANT AND overbearing - every one of them! She slammed the door closed behind her. It was just like Thomas Hale to think he could order her around like one of his crew. She wrapped her arms around herself as his reproach settled around her like dark clouds.

At the sound of a knock, Milly flung the door open, to find Will on the other side.

"You!" she simmered. "You did nothing to help my cause!" Her upper lip curled into a snarl. "And I thought we were friends!" She paused and her snarl melted away.

The pounding of Wills heart formed a desperate backbeat to the clanking of the pipes, and he felt a bead of sweat roll down the back of his neck. He exchanged looks with Milly.

He looked at her. "Oh no, our first fight!"

Milly glared at him. "I don't believe that's an accurate term since we aren't a couple." Then she stuck her tongue out at him, but there was no malice in the gesture. It made him chuckle.

He grinned. "Oh come on now … you have to admit it - that was funny!"

Will turned to leave, but he gave Milly hope when he spun back around and told her, "I think you'd best stay in your cabin for awhile. Don't worry - we will see that you make the trip with us."

TWO HOURS LATER, there was a knock on Milly's door.

"Come in," she called out.

The door opened and Yeager stepped inside with a triumphant expression written across his face.

"... So? What happened?" she asked, propping both elbows on her knees.

"Be ready at five o'clock tomorrow morning." He grinned, proudly. "I told *Captain Hale* that I was old enough to be his father, and I threatened to put him over my knee and paddle him until he came to his senses."

Milly sat straight up with a stunned look on her face. "Yeager! You didn't!"

"And why not? It's my right!" He leaned in close to Milly and said in a loud whisper, "Thomas Hale is my son."

Then he twisted an imaginary key in front of his mouth. "Mum's the word."

Chapter 40

WILL HELPED MILLY step down into the lifeboat and the others joined them. The chains of the davits rattled as they lowered them into the waves, soon releasing the boat, leaving it rocking in the water.

Short and wiry with a ruddy complexion and small suspicious eyes, the ship's mechanic, Tim, was not amused. "Damned fool's errand!"

After four long hours of braving the ocean current, trying to make sense of Will's convoluted map, Captain Hale cleared his throat. "Are you sure there really is an island that you were on out here, *fly girl?*"

"So!" shrieked Milly. "You think I … I'm out here for *fun?*" She swept her arm at the roiling water.

A tern flashed by them in the shadowy sky. As if on cue, their eyes followed as the bird returned, circling above them in a counter-clockwise direction. Will's face paled. He opened and shut his mouth as if he were gasping for air.

The bright clouds of sunrise had cleared away leaving a brilliant blue sky. Behind Milly, in the distance, separating her from an obscure image of a tiny island far off in the distance, the sea surface had only an occasional white cap …

… and an intermittent, quick glimpse of something bobbing up and down in the water.

Captain Hale stood, but he sat back down. Milly saw the look in his eyes as he asked her, "Is that your plane, Susie?"

This time, she didn't bother to correct him. Her heart was beating too fast for her mouth to catch up with it. Milly's eyes widened as she studied the horizon, but she saw nothing.

Far off in the distance, in the water, Will could see a debris field of man-made objects. A rectangle and some round shapes that could be tires, along with a few other objects he could not identify.

"You see it? Where? Where is it?" Milly looked full circle.

Hale pointed off to the left. "There." Metal pieces, some charred or covered in dark seaweed, possibly from a wing, played hide and seek with them in the water.

And then Will turned Milly so that she was facing the opposite direction. "And there." An engine set nearly up right, exhaust tubes buried under the surface of the water, the propeller facing the sky.

He pointed off to the left wing, where the tail light bobbed upside down, next to the vertical stabilizer. "And over there."

Captain Hale dropped his binoculars to his side. "I'll be damned," he said, his tone laced with heavy sarcasm. "That just goes to show that you never know what you're going to find when you keep your eyes open."

Milly smiled. She tried to stay calm, but her nerves were prickling like porcupine quills.

Tim questioned her. "I thought you said you went down on land."

"We did. The Electra was damaged on landing, because we were very close to the reef, which was full of holes and rocks. A few days after the landing, the surf overcame the plane. I only caught little glimpses of her off and on, after that."

Captain Hale raised an eyebrow. "You think the current dragged her out to sea? That doesn't make sense. Airplanes don't make very good boats. I assume that your fuel tanks were vented, which means that the air would have emptied out very quickly, and the sea should have claimed her."

"It doesn't matter how it got there," Will said, as they approached the fuselage, bobbing up and down in the foamy waves.

Hale hastily ducked as a gigantic wave came sweeping over the edge, washing over them. It took a few minutes, but after they regained their direction and equilibrium, they stared at each other, in shock, then out at the rough water.

Gone. All of it. The pieces of the Electra had vanished.

Will was convinced that it was all really still there. It had to be! Maybe everything had just taken a dip under the water's surface.

"The sea giveth and the sea taketh away …," Hale breathed.

Another glance around, and then Will leaned forward, drops of perspiration rolling down the sides of his face. "That's just hooey!"

His eyes searched the horizon, and then he hastily jumped into the freezing water, treaded for a few seconds to get his bearings, then he swam toward where the wreckage had been, in a fast, determined crawl.

The fragments of the Electra were nowhere in sight. He dove under, where he had last seen the propeller. A big fish darted past his arm. Then another.

It took three tries and he flailed around with his arms, but finally, one of his hands grazed something uneven, near the rear of the plane - something metal with rivets in a pattern. His hands grazed over the bumpy rivets and along the twisted and cracked frame that was loosely holding it into place.

Suddenly he was falling, the black, frothy water coming at him. Pain surged in his arm and traveled to his chest. His body pulled downward. He became disoriented. Everything was dark. Which way was up?

The crew watched anxiously from the lifeboat, white knuckles gripping the sides, not daring to breathe.

And then Will disappeared.

YEAGER DID HIS best to comfort Milly, but it was difficult to console her when he was almost as upset as she was. She wept and then her brain tried to reason that he couldn't be dead. But in the end, her heart carried more weight. And she cried some more.

WILL HEARD A voice calling to him from above the water. It was yelling at him. He became intensely aware. Aware that there was something he must do.

Propel myself upward! Yes, that's it!

His head rose above the water. He gasped, choking as the vessel rowed closer to him. But when they pulled him back into the lifeboat, he was unconscious. He lay lifeless on the floor. And they waited.

It seemed to be taking forever for him to come back. Not like the other times. They wondered if this might just be his *time*. Milly's eyes welled with tears.

All they could do was hope.

His mind drifted to the past, and to the moments of his youth and his regrets. His whole body filled with powerful emotion. His mind was a jerky panorama of scenes.

"Confounded pest!" Yeager grumbled, sweeping his hand over his right ear.

A tiny movement off to Yeager's right caught Milly's eye. A set of miniscule wings, sporting a fleck of bright orange, darting back and forth between Will and Yeager, finally rested on Will's nose.

They watched Will's face turn from stone gray to warm pink. Milly watched his chest rise and fall slowly, with shallow breaths. Then he wrinkled his nose, reached up and smacked his face, sending the fly to the floor of the dinghy.

The first thing Will saw when he opened his eyes was Milly's smile. But there was little time to take much pleasure in the sight.

She leaned over, close to him. "You scared me. Don't ever do that again."

"… your plane …"

But she cut him off. "I don't care about the plane, if it means putting my friends … *you* … in jeopardy."

Will tried to finish his sentence. "But …"

Thomas leaned over Will and interrupted. "Where the devil did you go, Stockton?"

Will looked at him with surprise. "You saw me swim out to find Milly's plane."

"Yes, but when you couldn't locate it, why didn't you come back right away?"

Will sat up, almost immediately regaining all of his strength. He looked at Hale like he thought he'd lost his mind. "What are you talking about, Hale? I was only out there for a few minutes!"

"Damn it, Stockton! This is no time for games! We have been searching for you for hours! You cannot go missing in the water for that long and not expect us to think the worst!

156

Yeager stepped in. "Okay – the two of you just stop bickering like two old ladies!" He turned to Will. "Now, what can you remember, after you jumped in the water?"

"I reached out as far as I could toward the window of the plane, but it kept disappearing. I tried one last time, when it reappeared, to grab the panel above it. I barely touched the rivets … and it sent a shock through my whole body – like an electrical shock."

Will's head was suddenly flooded with questions from every direction.

"Will - You saw the Electra?"

"But it's all gone."

"Do you think you were hit by lightning, Will?"

Will squeezed his eyes shut and he sat up. The hairs on the back of his neck stood at attention. He raised his hand and pointed behind Hale.

The Electra was back.

Chapter 41

"FAR BE IT from me to upset your cockamamie plan, but I would like to assist, if I might. ...." Milly said in utter frustration, but they didn't pay any attention to her.

"We could sure use somebody else to go down with you, Will, and inspect what's out there."

She did everything but Rhumba in front of them, trying to get their attention as they sat at the dining table that evening, before retiring. Finally, she stood on a chair, placed her fingers in her mouth and she gave out a loud taxi whistle.

You could have heard a pin drop. They turned to face her.

Annoyed, Captain Hale huffed, "*Now* what do you want, Susie?"

"I have been trying to tell you that I can dive."

"You?"

"Yes. I have done it several times. And while I'll admit I am not an expert, I know what I am doing."

Hale's jaw dropped. This *new breed of woman* was going to take some getting used to.

A TERN CAWED overhead and she glanced up, watching it glide on the breeze.

Will stumbled for words, flattening his body and spreading his arms and he hit the water with a slap, sending silver droplets skyward.

"How graceful." Milly laughed briefly, then she took a quick breath and she dropped in after him. The cold water was like a vise at her torso, gripping at her hips.

Bubbles rippled around them as they vanished beneath the surface, and then only a fleeting trail of foam was visible.

Will kept an eye on his depth as he followed the rope down. He didn't want to stir up a lot of debris.

The current took him by surprise, at first, but he took off, descending further toward the shadow under the water's surface, feeling the tightening of his muscles as they worked to propel him downward.

An object materialized beneath him. He barely had time to stop himself from swimming into the side of the cockpit, hovering just under the water's surface.

Will slowed and let Milly arrive at the site first. She turned her head as she approached it, and he could almost feel her heartbeat when she knew there was no doubt that it was part of the Electra.

Will motioned for her to surface for air again, and she nodded, following his lead.

He shouted, "Well, What do you think?"

Her euphoria was unmistakable as she shouted back, "Yes!" Milly dove back down, several more times, until Will insisted she return to the boat and rest.

Eventually, when her legs began to stiffen from the exertion and the cold, she slowed and swam parallel to the weather-beaten lifeboat.

Holding on to the side, she was ecstatic! "Will, that's the Electra! I am sure of it!"

But Will was worried. He formed his words carefully, so as to cushion the blow as much as he could before he spoke. "Milly, I am not as sure as you are."

"Why?"

He told her about the sheet of metal riveted over what he thought should have been a door or a window. It didn't match with the Electra's design, from the picture in the newspaper.

When he mentioned the possibility that it might not be her plane, based on his findings, she explained that there was actually a patch made to cover a window that had been damaged after a bad landing in

Miami, earlier on her trip. That piece of unmatching metal, riveted to the body of the aircraft, was actually the very reason she was able to positively identify it.

Chapter 42

DETERMINED TO PUT the pieces of *Humpty Dumpty* back together again, it was decided that they must drag various waterlogged pieces of the Electra to the island for further study. And also that it was the only feasible place with a chance for having a location for a successful take-off.

Although some of the repair and assembly would take place aboard the *Compass Rose*, Captain Hale, Tim and Will discussed ferrying the fuselage and damaged wing separately and performing the final assembly of the Electra on shore. They determined that some sort of scaffolding would have to be constructed to raise the wing high enough to line up the bolts perfectly.

ARE YOU SURE you are ready for this? To return to that island?" The look on her face answered for her.

As they approached, Milly noticed that the island had turned brown while she had been gone. The sharp sea air and the waves whispered with memories. How long had it really been?

THE WATER SURGED and receded, each pass trying to knock them off their feet while simultaneously burying them and parts of the Electra deeper in the sand. Will stood and he wondered how long he would have to stand there before his entire body would be buried. He tasted the salt of the ocean on his lips; he was standing in the Pacific Ocean. *Impossible.*

A few smaller pieces from the plane, barely visible, strung out like ghostlings of a giant underwater creature seemed to rise and sink with the voracity of the tide.

"I remember this." She sloshed slowly through the reef, onto the shore. "The feel of the sun. The smell and taste. But it's different now."

DAYS WENT BY with their bodies exhausted, their minds focused on the Electra and their eyes averted from the scattered fragments. The prop. The engine. The mag. The altimeter, a few cables, the rudder, one wheel. They had to wrestle the engine onto a skid and drag it closer to the *Compass Rose*, where it would be brought aboard to be repaired and taken back to the island.

Chapter 43

THE FOLLOWING WEEKS were grueling as they salvaged what they could and brought pieces back to the island, hoping they could fashion things to make the Electra viable again.

Flipped with its belly exposed, the plane was righted by an unbelievable arrangement of cables and winches from the *Compass Rose.*

Working together, they began taking key parts back to the *Compass Rose,* to be repaired.

Hale stood at the rail, watching his crew as they scaled the fuselage, inspecting and picking apart the Electra.

Milly caught up with Hale, just as he was getting ready to leave. She was overwhelmed with gratitude. She touched his arm gently. "I don't know how I can ever thank you."

"Don't thank us yet. We haven't even pulled the left prop yet. We'll have to bring the hub back over to the *Compass Rose* to be rebuilt."

The crane hoisted the engine up and over, onto the deck.

And there it sat.

Where were they going to start?

THEY DISASSEMBLED THE engine, laying its fragments in an orderly fashion, on the upper deck.

Will stewed about the engine. He was replacing spark plugs and setting gaps when Milly joined them.

Will leaned in and got to work, with Harold and Tim, picking it apart and putting it back together again. And the more he fiddled with it, the madder he got.

Harold, the engineer of the *Compass Rose*, stared at the parts spread out in front of him, his chest heavy with the challenge that lay ahead of them. Monkey wrench poised, he spoke, his tone gentle for such a big man. "This is going to be a real challenge."

"I don't know how we will transport all of this back to the island, once we put things together."

"It's a *flying coffin*," grumbled Tim, the mechanic, as he wiped his sweaty palms on his trousers.

Tim's aunt had raised him. A fear-ridden neurotic, she had tried to instill in him fear of the dark, fear of strangers, fear of boats and planes, and fear of animals.

Yet here he was, in the middle of nowhere, at nightfall, repairing a plane, on a ship with a bunch of strangers and two dogs. Ironic.

Milly ignored him. Defiance flashed in her eyes. "Mind if I watch?"

"What would you know about this?"

"You might be surprised." She sat down in the chair by the door. "I also studied to be a mechanic."

Hale heard her from the upper deck and shouted down, "Is there nothing you haven't done, woman? Either you have had a very crowded life, or you are the greatest storyteller of the century!"

Milly addressed Tim again, completely ignoring Hale's commentary. "I won't get in your way."

Tim didn't look up. "Suit yourself."

Then she asked curiously, "Are you always this intense?"

"It depends on the job. This one seems to require it."

They fell into silence after that. The implications were clear.

WILL GRABBED A wrench and tossed it into a wooden crate. "Going to the island."

"That looks heavy," Milly said as Will hoisted the box onto the lifeboat.

"Tools of the trade," he replied. "Necessary, if we are going to get your plane in the air again."

Milly lowered herself down into the boat beside him.

Secretly he admired the fire he saw in her eyes, but he was also afraid for her. What if it didn't work?

Chapter 44

THE FIRST LIGHT of morning, one week to the day, started with the loading of parts from the Electra.

"Are you sure that this is permitted? Taking things back to the island after we've worked on them?" Morgan asked.

"According to the log – yes. But we cannot remain on the island overnight. All hands must be back on board by midnight," Will answered.

"Why? Will we turn into pumpkins?" Yeager asked sarcastically.

"The log states that we may go on land, but it can be only temporary … and for a good reason." Will told him.

"Who the hell decides whether it's a good reason or not?"

Hale faced them. "The bigger question is," he paused, "how are we going to get all of this off the *Compass Rose* and onto the island?"

CAPTAIN HALE OBSERVED as Will's idea came to fruition.

The *Compass Rose* carried six lifeboats with her. Two were hoisted over the rail, then lowered into the water and lashed together side-by-side. Next, two more boats were lowered and lashed together the same way. One pair of lifeboats was drawn up behind the other. The two pairs were then secured together.

169

Milly stood and beamed as she tightened the last knot. "Like a team of four horses harnessed to pull a stagecoach!"

Long planks of wood were passed over the side of the *Compass Rose* and placed along the gunwales of the joined lifeboats. The crew worked as the rain started to fall. Hale suggested they take a break, but they refused. They continued working through the night and into the early hours of the morning.

When they were finished, Captain Hale stared out into the ocean, in amazement, where a large raft had been constructed. One platform was about 6 feet long and 6 feet wide, but there was enough room for two men to get in the front of each of the supporting lifeboats and row. Other crew could sit and row at the stern of each of the two supporting lifeboats in the rear.

"Stockton, your ingenuity never ceases to amaze me."

Working in the cold all night long, the company needed rest. The work crew was called back aboard the *Compass Rose*; they caught a few hours sleep and were roused at noon. After lunch, the fuselage of the Electra was raised from the forward hold.

The steam winch was swiveled into position over the forward hold of the *Compass Rose*, and the wingless fuselage of the Electra was raised out of the hold, swung over the side, and lowered onto the raft.

Naturally, William Stockton supervised the operation. He was actually raised up with the plane, to make sure nothing went wrong. Will clung to the nose of the Electra and, with a rumble of gears and chains, the aircraft was slowly hauled out of the darkness. Whenever the dangling plane swung too close to the wall of the hold or spun out of alignment with the opening high above, Will averted collisions with a swift and timely kick.

Meanwhile, he held on for dear life, like *the General*, his favorite movie star, in one of his daredevil onscreen feats.

THE FUSELAGE WAS lowered into the raft in a blinding storm. The raft was positioned with the nose of the Electra facing the hull of the *Compass Rose*. The steam crane, puffing smoke, lowered the damaged wing down over the side of the ship and onto the raft.

When Will gave the signal, the rowers began to stroke, and the makeshift pontoon floated out behind the dinghy.

A team of two was dispatched to the shore of the island in the fifth boat that had been equipped with an outboard motor that had mysteriously and miraculously appeared on the deck while the company slept. Their job was to prepare a make shift landing ramp. With pickaxes, they chopped away at the rocks and jagged reef along the beach and hewed out an incline that led out to the sea.

AS THE MORNING hours slipped into afternoon, the crew began gathering more wood for their nightly campfire. It would only be a few hours until dusk and hunger was settling in. And although every meal Yeager prepared for them was appreciated, somehow everything seemed to taste better over campfire.

Chapter 45

"I KNOW WHAT we could do!" Milly jumped up and said. She quickly rummaged through the cabinets, then darted to the refrigerator, in pursuit of something, what, Yeager didn't know.

"When I asked you what I could do to help, I never expected this," Yeager said with a grumble. He took the box from Milly and lowered it into the lifeboat, along with the supplies for dinner. He smiled and he helped her into the boat behind him.

"SUPPER IS AS tasty as ever, Yeager," Will said as he took a forkful of potatoes.

Yeager opened the lid of the steaming pot, then juggled the hot cobs into a spare plate. Peeling back an edge of the husk, he saw that the glossy kernels of corn had turned a warm gold. He offered one to Will.

Will spread a lump of butter over one of the corncobs, and bit into it, his mouth filling with the sugary, nutty flavor. He finished half the corncob and then wiped the butter from his lips with a napkin.

Milly eyed them, waiting until they all had finished eating. "Anyone ready for dessert?"

Captain Hale looked at Yeager with wide eyes, his tongue practically hanging out of his mouth. *"Cherry Cobbler,* Yeager?"

But Yeager shook his head and rolled his eyes, deferring to Milly, who was already on her feet, rummaging through the crate she and Yeager had brought over from the ship. She motioned to them all. "Now, everybody come over here and take one of these paper sacks I have prepared.

One by one, they grudgingly walked over to the box and took out a bag. Will peered in his bag and pulled out a graham cracker. He looked puzzled.

Milly laughed at his expression and reached in the bag. She took out the rest of it. She grinned from ear to ear.

"Marshmallow and chocolate?" Hale asked. "Why would I want this?"

"You're going to make a *S'more.*"

"A what?"

"It's called a *S'more.*"

Milly giggled and began her tutorial. "First, you toast your marshmallows." She handed them each a thin stick and demonstrated how to skewer two marshmallows on them.

Milly heard minor grumbling from the ranks, but it didn't bother her in the least. "Does she think we have never toasted marshmallows before?"

She held hers over the campfire. After a few minutes, she moved her stick away from the fire. Each marshmallow was perfectly golden, the toasted sugar-skins breaking to reveal melting white interiors.

"Now you take one of these crackers and place a marshmallow on it." Then she reached over and broke the chocolate bar in two, topping the marshmallow. They watched as the chocolate bar softened to a gooey state and she then put the remaining graham cracker on top.

And she had created a chocolate bar sandwich. She took a bite and delighted while the melted marshmallow and chocolate squished out around the sides and ran down her arm.

They laughed at her, but it didn't take long for them each to try their hand at making their own *S'mores.*

As Milly was finishing her last bite, Will caught her eye and sat next to her by the fire. "Let me taste." Having noticed a bit left on her thumb, he took it into his mouth and licked off the sticky sweetness. She blushed.

An overwhelming wave of a sense of accomplishment washed over them as the crew finished their dessert.

But it was short-lived. As they discussed their final check, it was discovered that they were missing a few extra supports for the track - to keep the wheels from digging further into the sand.

And they had depleted all of the viable lumber they had.

Will gathered the oars and leaned them against a tree. He exhaled a loud huff of frustration. He noticed Milly, still at the campfire, and sat next to her. She smiled back at him and nodded, light from the campfire and excitement flickering in her eyes.

He explained as best he could to her, the new wrinkle in their plan. "We don't have anything strong enough to do the trick, Milly."

But as he went on, she grinned and Will saw more than excitement mirroring in her eyes. In her eyes, he saw another reflection.

They had missed it - there was one more stockpile of lumber available. The oars from the lifeboats.

"I can see the wheels turning," he said, laughing.

"Do you really think it's possible?"

He looked philosophical for a moment. "Of course it's possible!"

THEY WERE HAVING so much fun, making and devouring *S'mores*, and discussing how they could use the oars, that they lost track of what time it was.

"Will, are we going to make it back before midnight?"

He nodded with a smile. "Of course we will!" He faced away from Milly to keep her from seeing the frown of worry on his face.

He had no idea what time it was.

JUST OUTSIDE THE door of each cabin the next morning sat a large, round, orange pumpkin. To which nobody claimed responsibility for.

Chapter 46

HE SAVORED THE invigorating moment of completion.

Captain Hale shook the hand of every man in his company, and he slapped Will on the back. "Now then, who have we designated to be our guinea pig?"

Milly jumped in, interrupting. *"Me!"*

Thomas Hale cringed, but he knew better than to argue with Milly. He had learned his lesson.

Will turned to her. "We don't know how safe it is yet… we can't put you at risk."

"Oh, I don't mind," Milly said. "Somebody has to do it – it's my plane. It might as well be me." She looked away as she snapped the button on her flying cap.

She continued with a wink. "Some risks are worth taking." Her tone and her smile let him know she was referring to more than the flight on the horizon.

BY THE TIME Milly caught up with them later, the project was already in test mode. She ran toward the sound - it was absolute music to her ears.

The Electra strained to rush forward. The engines roared, the fuselage shook, and the two spinning propellers were medallions of blur.

ENGINE CHECKED, SPARK plugs cleaned, fuel pump fixed - and autopilot repaired. He rubbed the kinks from his neck as he reviewed their work.

Hope filled her eyes.

Yeager took her elbow and propelled her toward the plane.

"I'm not certain what will happen." She caught a sideways glance at Will, deep in thought. "I'm not scared," Milly slipped on her goggles and gloves, "But I am … cautious."

The crew of the *Compass Rose* just hoped the wings wouldn't fall off completely.

Milly aimed the plane into the wind at the end of the island. She throttled up and took off down the island coast.

Will wasn't even sure she would make it to the reef. The consensus among the crew of the *Compass Rose* was that the Electra might nose over and wind up on her back. This scenario, of course, assumed that Milly could gain speed.

She lumbered along for a while, the length of a football field, before the screaming engines developed full power. Gradually, the Electra picked up speed. Beyond the point where the smooth, hard-packed sand runway ended, she could see a trackless terrain of loose coral and jagged seashells leading to the Pacific.

The engine ran but did not generate enough power to keep the aircraft in the air. She was 10 miles an hour short of her rotation speed when, she saw, up ahead, the hard-packed sand just about gave way to the jagged reef. She knew it was no use - it would slow down once she got into the wet sand and wind up having to be fished out of the water again.

A lead wave of the surf reared from the sea. It sucked up the water in its path, exposing the reef, jagged and brittle like the carcass of a chicken from which the meat had been sucked clean. The wave broke with a thunderous boom that reverberated in her chest. Water splintered across the serrated reef.

Another wave stormed in, sucking the reef raw and exposing new patches of jagged coral. Her heart raced. Her headache pounded. She had to remind herself to breathe.

But when she pushed the throttles forward, the plane swerved to the right and buried its nose in the sand. She throttled back the engines, and the Electra plunged deeper into the sand, but her skill and experience prevented her from nosing over before she came to another complete stop.

THE FOLLOWING MORNING, they returned to the site of where the plane was resting.

The Electra stood angled in the middle of the reef with its cockpit hood yawning open. From beneath the hood came a series of thugs and grunts. After a bit, a wrench fell into the surf with a resounding splash.

Will muttered something unintelligible, stood back and swabbed his forehead with a greasy rag from his rear pocket.

He frowned. The Electra couldn't be taxied through the 100 yard wide reef to the edge of the water. And it couldn't be dragged out of the water until its weight was reduced.

Cans of gasoline were removed and the wing and cabin tanks were drained, the fuel siphoned back into the steel drums. Tim estimated that it had brought down the weight of the plane by about two tons.

It had baffled and befuddled them when the drum of fuel appeared on the island, sitting in the reef, the morning that they brought over the repaired propeller from the *Compass Rose*. But they didn't question it for long – they had learned long ago that they were given exactly what they needed. No more, no less. So they gratefully accepted it.

WILL WIPED THE wrench against his thigh, and then he went after the propeller, tightening everything with Herculean effort. It occurred to him that he might pay for this later - that somewhere along the line, he might have to remove these bolts again, but he didn't care.

A voice broke his intense concentration. "Will, you have done everything you can possibly do ...*twice!"* Milly handed him a canteen of water.

He wailed into another bolt, then another, not wanting to discuss it. Will ducked out from the innards of the plane and smeared what he could of the grease from his hands.

Even though he knew it wasn't true, Will couldn't rid himself of the feeling that this could have been prevented, and that he'd made some mistake - that he'd missed something that kept her from getting off the reef.

With one rotation of his knuckles, he crushed the metal clamp and smashed the last hose into place.

THE MECHANICAL SYSTEMS had been checked and rechecked. The only question raised was about the human operator. Milly wanted to take off immediately, but Captain Hale and Will insisted that they all get a full nights' sleep.

Milly frowned but a compromise was reached. They would all go back to the *Compass Rose* and sleep for four hours.

The sun had long gone down, but she was too giddy to sleep.

Tim cut the engine and exited the cockpit. This time, Will and Hale had agreed, it was do or die.

Chapter 47

EXCITEMENT SURGED THROUGH her. Milly opened her eyes wide as a thought occurred to her. She approached the plane and tightened her scarf. She shot Will a playful grin. "Where would you like to go?"

Will's jaw dropped. He looked shocked. "Me? What do you mean, Milly?"

"You said it was a dream of yours to fly. You said you've never flown in an airplane. Come with me."

The warmth of the morning sun settled into his abdomen at the assurance in her face. He put the small wrench in his pocket and aimed his face toward the sun. He smiled at the vastness of the sky.

"Well, at least for awhile - I'll bring you right back." She mumbled under her breath, "If I can."

ALTHOUGH SHE REMAINED in complete control of her faculties, she didn't breathe comfortably until she was in the plane, starting the engine.

When the engines were fully engaged, and Milly felt the heartbeat of the Electra, she nodded to Tim who then slowly backed away. The plane bolted down the shoveled out, hole-filled, uneven reef strip.

Milly, head bent slightly forward, her eyes glued to the instrument panel, set her jaw.

They could soon feel the wings beginning to carry more and more of the weight of the Electra; they knew they were going to get out of the water. Milly smiled at Will the instant they did.

They continued to gain speed. Milly gave it more gas. The plane suddenly separated, and she pulled back on the wheel.

The plane lifted into the air, wheels going silent, the deck giving way to silky smoothness. They started to climb. Will watched as they gained altitude. He hoped his time in the air would help clear his head ... and his heart. His life was suddenly feeling as if it were being held together by as many wires as the Electra and, one by one, they were snapping free. As the plane rose in the sky, he leaned back and closed his eyes.

The crew of the *Compass Rose* had been watching the plane waver, then finally take flight. There was an overwhelming, shared sense of relief and satisfaction at a job well done.

The engine rumbled, and Will opened his eyes in wonder. Ascending into the low-lying clouds, the suddenness caught him by surprise and he elicited a soft gasp. The sky was so huge, so vast it seemed to stretch out into infinity. In light of such power, he felt his own relative smallness. An idiotic smile stretched his lips from one end to the other.

Milly banked sharply away and pulled back on the wheel. "I want to do a circle, and then we'll get up and away and into some fresh sky."

They soared above the island. The land beneath them dropped off. Will saw a big wide ravine with steep slopes, lined on both sides with grass and trees. A narrow river cut a thick dark line down the middle.

Will had come to appreciate water. It was beautiful. All along the river, he could see colorful vegetation and animals, many of them stopping to gaze up at them in awe.

Milly grinned. What a glorious sensation to be in the air after all that work! Then, with an almost impish gleam in her eyes, she suddenly called out, "You take the controls."

"What?"

"Take the wheel!" She grinned.

"I - I can't!"

"Why not? You want to learn, don't you? The most effective way to do it ... *is to do it.!"*

"You fly!" Milly shouted. "You can do it!"

Will leaned over, reaching with his left hand. Her hand was still on the wheel, but he grasped it, just above hers, and for a moment both their hands were flying the plane, steering their path together. His breathing quickened.

Then she let go. And Will was flying the plane himself. At first so smoothly, he was unaware of what he was really doing. And then, he was very aware - aware that he was, in fact, really flying an airplane!

"You're very comfortable up here," she said at last. "You're a good pilot!"

"You're not a bad passenger, yourself."

But before too long, Will sensed something was awry. They seemed to have hit some rough air and he had to concentrate on the controls to keep them steady. A southerly wind was buffeting the plane from side to side. The wind seemed to be pounding at the glass. Milly went quiet for a long stretch.

Suddenly, a loud and sustained vibration shook the plane. The bolts anchoring one of the cowlings to the fuselage had torn loose.

Will turned to Milly. "What's wrong?"

Her reply was drowned out by the wail of the wind, but he read the words from her lips. The air inside the plane suddenly felt heavy, pressing Will into his seat.

"I'm going to try to take us down over there!" Milly gestured to the ocean.

For a heavy object traveling at 50 or 60 mi an hour, water can be an exceptionally hard and resistant surface. And putting an aircraft equipped with wheels down on the choppy sea was nothing she had ever done.

But Milly was calm. She cut the engines. "We will be all right," she said. Her voice sounded dead into his ears, but still he was not afraid. He trusted Amelia Earhart, the woman who had conquered the sky in 1937, to bring him safely back to Earth.

She pulled back on the control wheel, gently raising the nose, as the aircraft coasted down, to allow the plane to settle.

With adrenaline tingling his every pore, Will nodded, holding on tight to the edge of the seat. As the sea came rushing up at them, he automatically ducked his head, feeling, not seeing, the plane hit the ocean. For a suspended breath, he thought they were fine - but then he felt something break beneath them.

She tried her best to land on the water, but they slammed into the surface of the sea with such an impact that the Electra began to splinter and fall apart.

Chapter 48

GRADUALLY, WILL WAS aware … he was in the ocean. Outside of the plane. He was out on the water, struggling - wrestling the current like he was riding a raging bull.

How had he gotten there? Where was Milly?

Will's insides turned cold until he caught a glimpse of the plane out of the corner of his eye. But as he neared it, the waves lapped over a wing, sinking it lower. Another wave rose, swelling beneath the broken Electra, lifting the plane high, then in a mighty rush, thrusting it so sharply that it almost capsized.

MILLY HAD BEEN still conscious when the plane first hit the water, but after a failed attempt at breaking the window, she had passed out. The darkness was absolute. She was unaware of anything.

Will took a deep breath. And he dove.

The plane wasn't completely submerged, but most of it was beneath the water's surface, and the sea was quickly gaining on it. The light from above shone down in the direction of the cockpit.

The beam picked up a pale hand, pressed against the glass, wisps of brown hair floating in the faint stream of light.

Feeling his way, he found the windshield and hammered the wrench against it as hard as he could. It didn't give. He pounded several more times. The glass was cracking and weakening, but not enough. He surfaced again for air. His chest felt heavy, his lungs began to burn.

Will dove back down again. He knew he was running out of time; the fuel had already begun seeping into the water around him. He kicked at the window again, but nothing was happening.

Then he remembered the riveted sheet of metal that covered the hole in the door at the back of the Electra. He swam, pulling himself along the body of the plane until he finally reached the door at the rear portside.

Will pried and wrenched at the frame that loosely secured the metal to the fuselage, splitting and separating the steel from the rivets. He anxiously watched water begin to seep in at a disturbing rate. He surfaced again for more air, then back down. There wasn't much time left. He widened the hole by kicking it until he was able to wedge his shoulders through it.

Back to the surface, he inhaled a long breath and held it. He went back under for what he hoped would be the last time.

Sharp shards scraped against his head and arms, but he ignored the pain. Will pulled himself through the inside of the plane, struggling, crawling and clawing at anything he could reach to pull him further toward the cockpit.

It was an amalgamation of metal and cords. Blindly, he groped for Milly and found her right arm. When he touched it, she didn't react.

His mind screamed. *God, no!*

His heart sped up. Where he had been sitting was nothing more than a mangle of shredded metal entwined with cloth. The seat had been severed in two, but there was no time for *what-ifs*. He shifted gears to Milly.

Will reached for her seat belt. It was unfastened; she had managed to do that. The sea continued to toss the Electra around in its wild current until finally, he was able to pull her free.

He hooked his hands under her arms and pulled her through the hole left by the absence of the riveted panel, carefully but quickly. Neither had much time left. He was out of air, and she was completely still.

Once he had her clear of the fuselage, he used his free arm and performed a hard scissor-kick to surface. His lungs screamed for oxygen. He kicked as hard as he could, but his limbs were becoming heavier by the second, rubbery and clumsy.

Will looked upward, to the surface - it looked like it was only a lighter shade of black. Still, he struggled toward it. Finally, his head broke the surface and he gulped a mouthful of air.

He knew Milly was in grave danger. Making sure her face was clear of the water, he began to swim, keeping her on her back. His body was still hungry for oxygen, and he was exhausted, but he slammed against the current as fast as he could. He swam, the heavy seas breaking over his head with every fresh wave.

Will kept his head above water, though he had to have swallowed at least a gallon of seawater as he struggled to propel Milly and himself through the waves.

With the seas thrusting him up and down, he assumed the men might have trouble finding them. He didn't see the lifeboat that had been dispatched the moment it had appeared they might be in trouble. So he set his sights on returning to the island.

When his feet touched the reef, he waded the rest of the way, then heaved himself up on to the beach, carrying Milly along with him.

"Come on, Milly," he said as he rhythmically pumped her chest. "Don't die on me now. You're not finished yet." Water trickled over his face into his eyes, but he didn't stop the compression or listening for some encouragement that she was alive.

What are you doing? It's not your time! Get back here!

But as he stared down at her lifeless body, his frustration eventually took on the impression of a dare.

"You told me you had more courage in your *little finger* than the rest of us combined. But this time, *you* are the one giving up here, *fly girl!*"

He turned away for a quick moment.

"Will." The voice was weak and hoarse.

She was still with him. She was alive!

AN HOUR LATER, Hale and Yeager greeted them in a lifeboat. After the vessel was in the safety of the davits, Hale tossed the line onto the deck of the *Compass Rose,* a good ten feet above them.

Yeager went aboard first. "Let me take your hand, Milly. High step up." Milly grasped Yeager's firm hand and he pulled her up and over the railing.

She stood on the main deck of the *Compass Rose* with a cocky grin. "What a ride!" she said in a voice still weak and slightly out of breath, but excited.

The thrill of the flight was still fresh in Will's mind, but he was soon somber … silent. He was confused, disoriented, flooded with waves of guilt and anger. He sat on the deck in silence.

The crew of the *Compass Rose* stood still and watched. Milly moved first and crouched beside him. It was almost unbearable to face her, but he met her eyes. "Milly." His voice shook, his eyes blurry as he put an arm around her shoulders. "I'm sorry."

He stood and walked away from her, setting his gaze on Milly's plane, bobbing up and down in the water.

Milly caught up with him and gave his arm an impatient shake. "Thank you, Will. I just had to tell you," she said. "I thought you should know."

They watched from the starboard deck of the *Compass Rose,* with sadness, as the magnificent sea began to swallow the pieces of the Electra, one at a time.

Will said, "How foolish to believe we are more powerful than the sea or the sky." He brushed back the hair from Milly's eyes. Her heart skipped a beat as his fingers lingered on her skin.

Pleasure sparkled in her eyes. "We'll just go back to the drawing board and try again." She grinned.

He knew there wouldn't be another time. They had used up everything they had… on that one chance. "I'm afraid we put all our eggs in one basket, so to speak," he said. "I'm so sorry, Milly," he said with his head hung, and he walked away again.

Clenching her hands together, Milly stood off to one side, watching him pace, nervously. Then he leaned against the starboard railing.

She joined him. "What is it, Will?"

"I feel guilty."

She touched his shoulder. "Whatever for?"

"I'm sort of glad we crashed." His voice wavered. "I hated the thought of losing one of my best friends." He inhaled and let out his breath. His heart pounded in his chest at the audacity of his thoughts.

"Plus, I finally realized one of my biggest lifelong dreams - all thanks to you." Then he took her hands in his, not quite able to look directly at her. "But what about you, Milly?"

Her grayish eyes searched his face.

"It isn't fair. Don't you deserve the same? After all you've been through ..." He brushed at her silent tears, but more came. "...you're still stuck here."

"Maybe that's not so bad, Will. I have found quite the collection of friends here, haven't I?" She leaned forward and put her hands on his shoulders, giving him a quick kiss on the lips.

She smiled up at him. "You're my hero."

His suddenly searching dark eyes looked shocked. "What?"

She met his eyes with a crooked smile. "I said you are my hero."

Will shook his head, in silence.

"You are. Because of how strong you've been, and how you've reinvented yourself."

Milly leaned back against the railing beside him and crossed her arms across her chest. Will saw a quiet smile cross her lips. And then he realized that he was smiling too.

WILL'S HEAD BEGAN to spin - he lost his equilibrium. In the twilight between dream and reality, his head throbbed with unbearable pain. He heard something. A distant rolling thunder, gradually increasing in volume. A deafening, earthshaking roar so strong that he felt it in the depths of his chest.

He would have assumed they were headed into another storm, but the reverberation possessed an unfamiliar higher pitch that quickly morphed into a rough whoosh, followed by a bone-jarring rumble.

High in the sky, a formation of unfamiliar aircraft whizzed past, startling him out of his revelry. At least he thought they were planes – they were nothing like he had ever seen before. But they were in the sky, so he assumed they were planes.

Will stared into the heavens, mouth open as all hands scampered out onto the deck. Ear-splitting cacophony followed, during which they each tried, unsuccessfully, to outshout the other.

Will began to worry - wondered if they had stumbled into a battle of some sort – a war. Milly tented her hands over her eyes.

During his history lessons, Milly had told him that the US fleet flew by all the time in 1937 and that there was nothing to worry about, unless a siren was blaring.

No siren. Nonetheless, it shattered what was left of his nerves.

"Are they ours?" he shouted to Milly, as he covered his ears with his hands.

Chapter 49

IT WAS ALMOST directly above them. The loud throb of its engines resonated in his head and he clapped his hands over his ears.

"It's not a plane!" Hale shouted over the roar.

Or was it? Its wings were short and sloped backward.

Milly was stunned as the futuristic vehicle, assisted by jet engines, closed in right above them.

She had no idea what it was, but that didn't matter. She grinned and ran to meet it, practically catapulting to the bridge, letting her hands flap in the air to show her euphoria. She shouted down at them. "No, it doesn't look like any plane I've ever seen!"

Will stared upward as the sound of the engines rose. Within seconds, the jet began a slow, shaky descent, straight down, toward the deck of the *Compass Rose*, the back draft itself almost lifting them skyward.

Milly felt a little lightheaded as she tumbled down the steps to rejoin the others, as the aircraft made its landing. Yeager and Will ran to her aid.

If he hadn't seen it for himself, Will would have sworn that the plane was dropped down to them on strings, like a puppet. Milly stood and wavered slightly, and then she stumbled blindly, toward Will. He reached out and caught her just as her knees collapsed. "Milly! Are you alright?"

The plane settled. Engines stilled. An open cockpit revealed a man in a dark green jumpsuit. He climbed from the cockpit, and quickly leaped down. Carrying a clipboard, he approached the small group, staring at him in stunned silence. The company of the *Compass Rose* held a collective breath as he removed his helmet.

The pilot grinned at their reaction. "It's a *Harrier* jet. Pretty cool, isn't it?"

But they stared back blankly at the comment.

The man searched their faces and smiled again. He flipped over the top page of his clipboard. "Which one of you is Amelia?"

Yeager leaned over to Tim. "He's joking, right?"

Will gave her shoulders a light shake of encouragement. "Milly, that's you!"

Her legs seemed too weak to hold her up. The engines were racing - it was hard to catch her words. Milly, surprised that the man knew her name, returned to the real world and replied. "I-I-I am."

Will couldn't contain his excitement. He wasn't sure which he was more excited for - Milly, because he sensed she was finally about to see her dream through, or for himself - previewing a glimpse of the future … and dare he imagine … *space travel?* He locked eyes with Milly.

For several heart-pounding moments, neither of them spoke but only stared into each other's eyes. The intensity in his expression held her bound.

Milly ran her hand over the rail as she walked past the cargo holds on the deck of the *Compass Rose*, toward the waiting aircraft. Her grayish eyes twinkled as they began to mist over. She gazed back at Will. "The *Compass Rose* has been my home for the last several weeks …"

She tilted her head to the side and looked back at the man waiting on the deck.

He nodded at her, as if to be granting her permission. "Take all the time you need," he said.

"I never understood that phrase – *take all the time you need.*" She approached Will and sighed. "What if I take more than I need? Or less? Would that be bad?"

Will brushed her hair away from her eyes. "I guess it means to take your time. Don't rush yourself."

"I never imagined it would be so hard to say goodbye to you all." Milly flicked a glance up at him - it was sad and hopeful all at the same time.

Will gave her a wink.

"You've been so wonderful – my safe haven in the storm." She walked past them all, touching each by the sleeve as she passed them. "I feel like I am losing my big brothers."

Captain Hale was first. He took her hand. "Milly …" He raised it to his lips and kissed it. "… I know we did not always agree on things, but I hope you know that I always had your best interest at heart."

Milly blushed and smiled. "Of course I know that, Thomas."

"I knew that you deserved better than living aboard a broken down vessel with her salty crew and a grumpy sea-captain."

She hugged him.

When she got to Yeager, she couldn't help noticing that the brackish old cook was hiding something behind his back.

"What have you got there, Yeager?" She smiled, straining to see around him.

He slowly presented a paper sack and placed it in her hands with a sheepish expression. "Thought you might get hungry."

Milly unrolled the top of the sack and peered inside. Tears instantly filled her eyes. In the bag was a can of beans – Yeager's *precious* beans!

"Oh Yeager – Thank you so much! I will cherish them." She looked away for a moment, wiping her tears, aware that he would view them as a weakness. "I'm sorry," she sniffed. She hugged him tightly.

The rigid tension in Yeager's bones seemed to melt and his face twisted. A tear stole out of his eye. He let out a heavy sigh.

But before he released her, he whispered to her, in that gruff voice that only Yeager was capable of. "Good to let sadness out. Makes more room for joy."

She kneeled beside Clancy, straightening out her collar. She scratched her behind the ears. Clancy immediately dropped to the deck for a tummy rub.

Milly laughed and obliged. "There now, Clancy - once in awhile, a lady must remember to play hard to get." Clancy flipped back over and Milly savored her scent as she rubbed her face in the amber colored fur.

As Milly stood, she clutched the chain around her neck, holding her ID tag. With a smile, she removed it and returned to Clancy's level. She carefully wrapped the chain around Clancy's leather collar, securing it. Then she grinned. "And jewelry. A girl has to have one basic piece of jewelry that will go with everything."

Milly's expression fell slightly as she realized that time and elements had worn most of her identification from the surface. "It's yours now." She frowned, with a note of disappointment in her voice. "I only wish it had your name on it."

But Will, sporting an ear-to-ear grin, stepped in and pulled a tiny knife from his pocket. He stooped down beside them. "Women have their jewelry … and men have their pocketknives." He scratched the letters on the flat side of the tag:

C-L-A-N-C-Y.

He stood and smiled. "It's a little crude, but it does …"

Milly interrupted him. "It's perfect!" She scratched Clancy behind her velvety ears.

She stood and smiled up at Will. "Will …" She hugged him. "I think I have not seen the last of you. And I can't wait to hear about your adventures!"

Will walked Milly slowly to the waiting aircraft. "Your chariot awaits, my dear." He patted his jacket pockets. "Oh, I almost forgot!" He reached in his coat and handed her the newspaper.

But Milly gently pushed it back toward him, with tears in her eyes. She took his hand gently in her own, managing to force a little smile for his benefit before she handed it back to him. "I think you are going to have far more use for this than I will."

Will glanced over Milly's shoulder at the streaks of light in the sky. He smiled down at her and cleared his throat. "Until then." When he looked into Milly's luminous eyes, he knew she felt the tug too.

Even though he hadn't known her for very long, he was feeling a great loss. He began to walk away, but Milly suddenly called out his name.

"Will!" She ran to him and leapt into his waiting arms. Her fingertips dug into his shoulders. They shared an emotional kiss.

He swallowed to ease the tightness of his throat. "I am going to miss you."

Milly rested her head against his chest. "I know that." She was silent for a moment, listening to his heartbeat beneath her ear." She could feel the tears sting her eyes. "I will miss you too. You are an amazing man, William Stockton."

"Not half as amazing as you are, Milly." His lips brushed her temple. "And don't forget it."

As he pulled back slightly, Will noticed that as Milly slid her arms from around his neck, her face was glowing in the afternoon sunlight and her hair had taken on the luster of 24-karat rose gold.

He reminded her, "Remember, it's all about the curve of the wind and the velocity."

"Flying?" She giggled. "Of course it is."

Will whispered parting words in her ear before releasing her. "I love you, Amelia."

Lights of the aircraft flashed, signaling it was time. She reached for his hand and held it tight for a moment, and she smiled. "I love you too."

He backed away from the jet. Her fingers tightened on the strap of her briefcase again. She twisted it around once, twice, until it was almost cutting off her circulation.

Milly made a get-on-with-it motion with her hand and Will laughed. She felt the breeze on her face as the engines of the harrier and her escort fleet, waiting in the sky overhead, rumbled louder.

The man motioned for Milly to step up and take a seat in the cockpit. But when she climbed into the jump seat, he shook his head.

"No ma'am. You are in the front."

She pulled herself into the front seat and she stared back at him, not understanding what he meant.

"This is a training jet. I am just your co-pilot ma'am." he said, as he positioned himself behind her.

Her eyes widened. Her heart beat erratically. "But ..."

"You'll know what to do." He handed her a helmet and he positioned his again over his head.

Under the direction of the voice coming from her helmet, Milly faced the aircraft into the wind. She listened to the voice, not really certain if it was coming from the earpiece in her headgear, or from somewhere else. She pulled the lever back to point the nozzles downward. She set the thrust vector to 90° and she brought the throttle up to maximum, at which point the aircraft began to push upward, everything in sight stirring from the downward jet blast. Then Milly trimmed the throttle until she had achieved a hover state at the desired altitude.

She had been secretly terrified of this moment: reaching the end of her journey and the fear of being on her own again. But as the harrier began to drift up, away from the *Compass Rose* and her family, the echo of wind and the rumble of waves fading, she realized that she wasn't leaving them behind; she was carrying them with her.

When she took a low pass over the *Compass Rose*, the crew cheered and waved. They weren't worried anymore about where she was going or anything going wrong. They sensed this was something they could count on - for Milly - a bridge to take her somewhere she had never been before, and they knew she couldn't wait to get there.

Chapter 50

NO LIGHT ON the horizon. It seemed a fitting phrase at this particular moment.

The fog rolled in, thick as a wet blanket. Even though it was late morning, the sun was blocked by clouds. But it would be only temporary.

It was just beginning to rain, long drops streaking down the window. Will took off his cap and angled his gaze toward the porthole, showing the hand lettered words Milly had written there, inside a heart that morning:

Thank you.

Despite everything, life seemed to go on, Will thought. He faced the breeze. He had to remind himself of that every day, find strength, even courage, in that knowledge.

After breakfast, he found himself on the portside deck.

"Depressed?" Hale asked as he approached.

"Yes." He stared into the darkness. "And angry."

Sadness crept into his heart. Milly was gone. God, he missed her! If there had been any chance at all that the two of them could have ended up together, it was gone now. Gone like the steam rising off the rails as the dampness of the night's rain evaporated.

"I am truly happy for Milly …" He paused, "… Amelia, Hale - I really am. But I do feel a great loss, you know." He patted his hands against the pockets of his pants, looking for something - a cigarette, he guessed- and seemed agitated when he couldn't find it.

"Time still passes, doesn't it? When we're not paying attention - while we're busy with other things, it just slips away. And then it's gone, and we can never get it back." He inhaled and let out his breath with his words. "I suppose I will eventually get over it. In time."

"It doesn't look like we have a timeline out here, Will." Hale gave him a look of melancholy and a sympathetic pat on the back. As he walked away, he added, "I have come to believe that the only reason for time is so that everything doesn't happen at once."

HALE POSITIONED THE calendar on the hook behind the door, flipped the page over and smiled to himself.

"I don't know why you even bother to advance the pages of the calendar, Thomas." Will leaned back in the swivel chair that had become his favorite spot on the *Compass Rose*, other than the Pilot House.

"You'd argue with a doorknob, Will Stockton." Hale said.

As he spoke, Will watched his face. He had learned that it was difficult to gage Hale's mood. But if you looked closely, you'd see clues - a twitch of the mouth, or his eyes twinkling behind the surface of his glasses when he was happy.

Above, the moon hung, hidden in a bank of clouds. The sphere itself was concealed, but its rays pierced through in a trail that extended from Heaven to Earth.

Hale continued. "Some people have a newspaper. I have my calendar."

"Touché."

THE NEXT FEW days dragged as if they were weeks. Yeager had prepared a special stew, using the spinach that had appeared in his kitchen that morning. Surprisingly, it seemed to offer a degree of comfort to him, and served as a reminder of Milly.

"Another beautiful day. Aren't we spoiled?" Yeager let out a chuckle as he passed them on his way to the kitchen.

Will faced Captain Hale. "Hale, I just want to have a normal, uncomplicated day."

"Normal?" Hale laughed. "You're the only person I know who would call *any day* aboard the *Compass Rose* a normal day."

After dinner, Will gathered Hubble and Clancy and set off on their nightly walk. As they approached the portside deck, he paused at the rail.

Only a small circle of stars remained visible in the sky. There was no sound except a faint distant rumble, coming closer. He looked up at the sky just in time to see the stars disappear. Clancy whimpered.

Frame shattering, the galley door flew open, banging loudly as a rush of wind whistled up from a nearby stairwell.

Something told him that this would be an excellent time to send the dogs to bed early. Making an about-face, he reached for the latch to open the compartment Clancy and Hubble called home.

Chapter 51

THE COMPASS ROSE. The terns and the water sang her song.

That afternoon, Will combed the *Plain Dealer*, studying the articles, constantly peeking over the top, to see if anyone was watching him, soaking in as much information as he could.

Will found himself wishing he could go back in time and listen more carefully, so he could write everything down so that the memories would never be forgotten.

Standing at the wheel, he finally arrived at a revelation:

We can never recreate the life - the dream; Things cannot be repeated, only done differently, but we loved and that must count for something.

It was the barking of the dogs that eventually drew him back to the present. He wasn't sure of how long he had been sitting on the floor with the newspaper in his lap.

Will wasn't sure if the day breezed by so quickly because he had lost the ability to track time, or if it was really changing. It was all so hard to gauge anymore.

Will pushed open the door, expecting Clancy and Hubble to rush him, but they weren't in their beds or at their food bowls.

He took a midnight stroll out along the deck. It had been some time since he had counted the stars; he'd lost all track of time. He took a deep breath and exhaled.

Will smiled at the sight of the two dogs on a pile of blankets together, asleep, near the bow of the *Compass Rose*. Clancy dwarfing Hubble, he couldn't help chuckling at the lopsided sight of the siblings.

Had his world ended? He grieved his past, present and future. He cleared his throat, moved by emotion.

Will stared up to the heavens, searching for the familiar constellations that, through the years, had always managed to get him through the roughest times of his life. He leaned against the rail, closed his eyes, and he did something he hadn't remembered doing before in his life – ever. He prayed for help.

FROTHY WAVES SURGED over the rails of the *Compass Rose*. The wind blew, a whistling in his ear that sounded like carefree laughter.

Will waited just outside the galley door, Clancy gave up a gruff bark, and the wind rushed across the deck. Will grabbed her by her collar and pulled her into the room. Then he set out to locate Hubble and bring him inside.

A tern swooped by them, calling out as it passed. Will searched the horizon, his hand making a visor for his eyes, wondering if just beyond it, heaven awaited. Might there be a place called eternity at that intersection of water and sky?

"It's a beautiful morning," Captain Hale said, as he passed him by. He looked out over the water.

Will stared blankly back at him.

Hale thought about it for a minute. "There's something important in this story, Will. Something that has the potential of touching a lot of lives, not just ours."

Still no response from Will.

"Everyone has dreams." He stopped and grinned. "Well, almost everyone. And everyone has known what it's like to see their dreams crumble - go unfulfilled. But these men - the twelve men left aboard the *Compass Rose*, have found something more stable to hang onto."

Will raised a brow at that.

"The legend."

"*Some legend.*" He threw his cigarette butt over the rail. "All of those dreams that can never come true," Will snickered.

"Will, you are missing the point."

"There is magic in the air surrounding us out here - magic in the fact that our dreams were not fulfilled because circumstances turned out the way we had hoped, but because of our faith in a legend that is above circumstance."

"Will we ever find a way to see our own dreams through and reconnect with our past lives? Where do we start?" Will asked.

Hale reached in his pocket and brought out a ring with 12 of the ship's keys on it. He held it by the largest, oldest brass key - the key to the wheelhouse. He jingled it. "I am optimistic, Stockton. The key, after all, is simple: *Go back to the original dream.*"

He tossed the keys to Will, who barely caught them before they sailed through the sky into the depths of Lake Erie. "Just think of what we have accomplished so far – the lives we have touched. The things we have changed, and …" Hale gave Will a wink and continued his thought. "…the dreams we have fulfilled for others."

It took him about an hour to cool off, but Will returned to the deck, where Hale was still staring out onto the horizon. "So, you believe that we are all being given another chance." Will pondered on that for a few moments.

Perhaps it was the opportunity of a lifetime, to find out if they could really make a difference. And amid all the conflicting emotions - the fear, the exhilaration, the apprehension, the sense of adventure - William Stockton knew that no matter what the outcome, dreams themselves were worth the risk.

It was all a gift. A frightening, uncertain, bewildering gift - but a gift, nevertheless.

Chapter 52

WILL WATCHED AS the Cleveland skyline came to meet them. It was different; some time in the future -- the tower was finished and much had been added to the skyline. Maybe 25 years or so, he guessed. But it was definitely Cleveland. It felt as though he'd been gone an eternity.

Maybe he had.

Thomas Hale came for him a few hours before sunset, followed closely by Hubble and Clancy. He uncapped the bottle and offered it to Will, who declined.

Will bent down and patted Hubble on the head. "These dogs have made such a difference out here. I don't want to lose either one of them." Will tangled his fingers in Clancy's fur. The pup whined.

The skyline came into focus as Hale brought his binoculars to his eyes. "Hubble is very happy … content with the way things are here, you know."

"Let me see." Will took the binoculars but the sun disappeared behind the clouds, making it impossible to make out much detail. He put down the binoculars and looked at Thomas. "What makes you so sure that this is going to work?"

Hale turned the binoculars slowly, between his hands. His expression betrayed a convoluted assortment of emotions.

In the distance, the city shimmered. Will threw his cigarette over the rail and waited for it to disappear.

"Let's get the hell off this godforsaken boat once and for all, and go home."

"We can't. You know that." Hale gave him a look of empathy. "At best, I believe you might be able to set foot on shore long enough to make sure the pup will be safe. But there is no guarantee."

That wasn't the answer he was hoping for, but what did he expect? He clenched his jaw and watched the dogs race across the deck after a tern. The sun was a ball of fire, slowly inching down toward the inky blue line of the horizon.

"But ..." Will said, in a raised voice, filled with anguish, staring across the harbor. "I'm not sure it's the best for her."

Captain Hale interrupted him. "At least that way, she will have a chance, Will. What kind of life is this for a healthy, live dog?"

A cold nose pressed against his leg. He reached out and touched her soft fur. "We have to let her go. She deserves a real life. I have a feeling that she will find a wonderful home; I'll bet there's a young boy out there who is just waiting for a best friend."

Heart in his throat, Will nodded to Hale in silent agreement. A tern, squawking, fluttered away, caught the breeze, circled back and settled again.

WILL FOLDED HIS hands across his chest and fought the sting in his eyes. With his anxiety mounting, he searched the shoreline. The current propelled them toward a rocky finger that jutted into Lake Erie. Captain Hale steered the lifeboat toward the shore.

Will stared out at the windswept beach at Edgewater.

"She's a good swimmer, Will. She won't have far to go." Thomas said.

"No. I will take her ashore myself."

Inhaling as he lit another cigarette. Hale said, "Are you willing to take that risk? You know that could place your personal destiny in jeopardy." Then he stared blankly out toward the horizon and continued. "Although I must say I expected this from you."

Will's heart sank, fighting the urge to be selfish, by keeping Clancy with him, aboard the *Compass Rose*. He had to get her to safety.

Clancy wasn't apprehensive at all about the ride in the dinghy - to her, it was another fun adventure - with Will. Her hair flowed and shined in the breeze from the lake. She knew enough to sit fairly still, remembering the time when, shortly after they had joined them, she and Hubble got so excited, they fell overboard. It hadn't seemed to bother Hubble much, but it had scared the daylights out of Clancy. Had it not been for Will, she might not have gotten back to the *Compass Rose*.

Will began to untie the dog's crudely scribed nametag from her collar, but Hale stopped him. "Let's keep that with her. Maybe whoever finds her will keep the name. She will always be our Clancy."

Will tied Clancy's collar to a rope and prompted her to jump out of the boat with him. They were just shy of the pier that John and Katie had spent so much time at - the dock where John had last been seen. Alive. He found it difficult to look at without so many memories flowing back to him.

He wondered again, what had been going through his brother's mind when he made the decision not to go on with his life. Will felt a strong pang of guilt - it was his fault. Had he not insisted on sailing with the *Compass Rose*, maybe everything would have unfolded differently.

Hale called out to him as the lifeboat retreated. "I will return for you in a few hours. Good luck!"

Will felt like he had stepped out into a little bit of heaven. He stared out at Edgewater. There were still jagged rocks, many of which he recognized, jutting from the cliffs by tufts of grass-covered earth. On the cliffs, here and there, were pockets of tiny wild roses that spilled down in miniature falls of color, as if holding onto summer as long as possible in their protected space.

The late afternoon breeze picked up and the little boats began to rock gently. The air was cooling off. Water lapped under the sturdy wooden pier, splashing against the pilings.

Will listened to waves breaking against the Edgewater cliffs, the wind circling the rocks, music carried on the breeze, sounding like an exquisite woodwind instrument. He closed his eyes and braced himself for a trip down memory lane.

Will stopped beside the dock. He bent over and studied a small rowboat tethered to the pier. It was old, its edges softened by time and weather; there was no way of knowing when it had been left.

It reminded him of John's old rowboat. He laughed. For as much money as he had, John could have had any boat he wanted. But he had insisted the old rowboat remain.

Clancy appeared to be slightly agitated. She was sensing Will's nervousness and reflecting in apprehension. He patted her on the head.

"It will be fine. You're a very smart girl."

Will allowed Clancy to explore a bit on her own, although he kept a close eye on her. He wanted to see for himself how well she would acclimate to a brand new life. A life with a completely different set of rules.

Clancy sniffed the ground cautiously at first. Soon she found herself bouncing back and forth, inspecting every rock, blade of grass, tree … and whatever else she spotted.

Will smiled as he watched her clumsily attempt to make friends with a butterfly then, just like a fickle woman, run off chasing the next beautiful thing she saw from the corner of her eye. He apprehensively took a few steps up - up to the rocky cliff, still keeping a watchful eye on Clancy on the beach below.

The path beside Will was overgrown with weeds and brush, but he continued the climb. He reached the street and stopped. He felt the thin veneer of his facemask crack when he saw what was in front of him.

There it was - John and Katie's house. He didn't dare get too close. Although he knew nobody would be able to see him, he just didn't think he could handle going back there, with all the history he had read in the newspaper, fresh in his head. No, it would be too painful. So he stood there, in silence.

To Will, the house was a metaphor of John and Katie's life together – spectacular, impractical, audacious, and benevolent.

Close by, he could see the weathered bench facing the lake and, by squinting, he made out someone sitting there. A man - a narrow, spindly frame, sitting quietly, just staring at the ground.

Maybe the magic newspaper had made a mistake. Or maybe he'd misunderstood the article about the Stockton Foundation. What if John was still alive?

He took a deep breath and started slowly toward the man sitting on the bench. But just as he got close enough to get a better look, he was startled by a voice coming from behind him.

"Elliott. Elliott!" When the man on the bench didn't answer, he boomed, *"Mr. Hutchinson!"*

Will's shoulders slumped. It wasn't John after all. It couldn't have been. And then he was hit with another dose of reality. The man approaching the bench was Jacques Laurent.

Jacques looked so different - not exactly an old man, but a little weathered and quite gray around the edges.

Had he really been gone that long? Will straightened and approached the bench, battling an odd combination of sorrow and anger.

He took his time surveying the area. Everything was silent; there was no one between the path and the bench. He continued walking slowly toward the bench - he kept his eyes fixed on the man sitting there. But before he could reach the bench, Jacques called out again.

"Elliott! It's time to go home!" He approached the bench and assisted the old man to his feet.

Will's shoulders drooped. He turned and walked back to the beach, dejected.

With Clancy in tow, he visited the dock again without knowing what he was looking for. He picked up a stick and instinctively threw it as far as he could throw it. Clancy took off after it, her tongue lolling. She came running back to Will with the stick. She dropped it at his feet and waited impatiently. Will tossed the stick in the opposite direction, sending Clancy off on a new quest, while he watched her leap and bound across the beach.

Will smiled, but there was a hint of something sad behind it. Hale was right - she needed to have a real life - a life with a place to run and play. A place - solid ground where she could roll around on her back, begging for a tummy rub. He inhaled deeply.

And that day would come.

But it wasn't today. Will could not leave her there, alone. He had to take the time to make sure she would be safe, warm and happy, before he would ever leave her behind.

So, when the sun began to set, Will attached Clancy's collar to the rope and they set off to the lifeboat, waiting for them at the dock, and set course for the *Compass Rose*.

As he settled into his bed that night, Will felt something warm and wet on his cheek. He smiled when he realized Clancy had licked him.

Chapter 53

WILL WAITED A day before returning to Edgewater Beach.

Clancy wandered up and laid her head on his knee. He scratched her behind her ears. "You have no idea how much I miss you already." He slowly backed away from her and tossed a stick in the air.

She leaped and landed with a skidding thump, her paws scrambling frantically to keep up with her body. She scampered, sending sand and dirt flying in all directions as she chased everything in sight.

There were more smells than her snout had ever smelled, more sounds than her ears could ever take in. She sniffed at the air. Her tail thumped to a wild rhythm.

Suddenly, she stopped. Light brown hair, catching glints of red in the afternoon sunlight.

Clancy went on point. *What's this? An unusually small human?*

She couldn't help staring. The ginger-haired boy was up ahead, walking from side to side, arms out for balance, kicking a stone.

Squirrels romping, birds of countless species fluttered overhead, but she seemed not to notice any of them - her eyes focused intensely on the boy approaching, eyeing him. Her heart thrummed wildly with each step he took toward her.

The boy dropped to his knees. He paused and waited for her to look over at him.

Should I run? Should I stay? Torn between decisions, she let out a confused whimper. *He must have me under some kind of spell.*

The boy sank as low to the ground as he could and slowly crawled toward Clancy, never breaking eye contact.

And to her surprise, she found herself doing the same.

When they got about an arm's length apart, the boy gently reached out and touched her.

Her instincts told her she should have been more cautious, but she just couldn't resist that face. She was drawn in closer by the scent of the boy, and whatever he'd had for lunch. While maintaining a slight distance, she licked his face, just to narrow it down, of course.

A cross between something slightly salty with a hint of smoke.

He giggled. "Hey, that tickles."

Will lifted the binoculars to his eyes before dropping them to his side and cast a backward glance at the dog and the boy on the shore, nodding as tears slipped from his eyes. He smiled.

Clancy continued to be pulled in, toward the boy, vacillating whether it was a good decision or not. The boy hastily reached out and grabbed her collar. Panic-stricken, she looked back at Will for help. She tensed and let out a frightened yelp.

Will jumped into action. He wanted to intervene, to take her by the collar and run – as fast as he could. Alive or not, she was *his* dog. What had he been thinking, leaving her all alone, in a strange place? But he took a few steps, and then he stopped. And he continued to observe from a distance. He held his breath.

The boy remained calm. In a voice just over a whisper, he said, "Don't worry. I'm not gonna hurt you." He reached out and ran his hand through her tangled coat. "It's okay."

Will let out his breath, not sure when he had been that young and carefree. He closed his eyes.

A sudden loud noise, coming from the parking lot, sent Clancy bolting back toward the beach.

"Aww, come back!" The boy kicked a stone across the path. His voice became quiet and sad as he continued, disappointment in his voice. "Why'd you have to go and do that? I wasn't gonna hurt you." He walked back toward the street, crestfallen, with his head down.

Will pondered for a few minutes. He was curious about the boy - what he was like - where he lived. Clancy seemed to like him and it was clear that the boy was infatuated with her.

But that was not enough for Will – he needed to see more. It needed more research. That was something that had been ingrained in him since childhood. Research.

He wanted to see where Clancy would be living – would there be a nice, soft and safe place for her to call home? Will was curious where the boy lived. How far from the shore of Edgewater?

He remembered the passage in the log that explained that there was a 5-mile radius from the deck of the *Compass Rose* – a safe zone, where, although he would be invisible to everyone, he might be able to venture a little bit farther on shore, without meeting his own demise.

And meeting his demise was not something he wanted to test – the book made it clear that if it's too soon, if it was not his "time," he would simply disappear; dissipate into thin air, without a trace. And it would be as if he'd never existed. He shook the thought from his head.

Depending where the boy lived, he just might be able to do it. He quickly spun around on his heels. The boy was already so far down the road that he doubted he would be able to catch up to him in time to see where he was going.

Out of the corner of his eye, Will spotted the car – an old jalopy, not unlike the new coupe John had bought just months before *the Compass Rose* had set out on its fateful trip in 1926. It was parked on the curb, with no other car in sight. He dashed over, Clancy on his tail and saw that the keys were in the ignition.

He hurried toward the car.

Could he do it? Would he remember how to drive it?

There wasn't time to think about it. He opened the front driver door and coaxed Clancy up onto the seat. Then he scooched in behind the steering wheel. He started the engine and Clancy's ears perked up at the thought of another new adventure.

He reversed the car and soon they were flying down the line of buildings and houses, and turning up the hill toward the city.

She kept climbing into his lap, but he had to keep pushing her back to the passenger side of the seat. Finally, he just gave up and drove slowly, with Clancy in his lap, one paw on the steering wheel, the other paw leaning out the open window, lolling her tongue in the breeze. She couldn't contain her excitement.

Will chuckled. "Clancy, you are a funny girl, you know that?"

Will leaned back, relaxed a little, and began to thoroughly enjoy the drive. His senses were heightened as his instincts kicked in and he shifted gears.

He perused the horizon, searching for the boy. He couldn't have gone that far – he just hoped he hadn't already made it home, already inside the house.

After a minute or two, Will began to get a weird sense. Was he being followed? But who could see him? By his estimation, there were only a few turns left on the way.

Whether he was being followed or not, he needed to act like nothing was wrong. *Just drive a block or take a couple turns, and see what happens.*

He took the first turn and slowed. His heart was beating hard. He took the second turn. *Calm down. Think. Where could the boy live?* He reached out for Clancy and patted her on the head.

As they approached a populated area on the street, Will began to feel eyes – watching, following them. Awestricken expressions.

Good God – can they see me?

It took Will a moment for the realization to set in that, no, they couldn't see him, but because they couldn't see *him*, they saw a *dog driving a car.*

Then the motor began to sputter. Swearing, he stamped his foot on the gas pedal, trying to make the car climb the hill. It did, catching well enough to make it, but a little past the road that ran down to the park, it simply caught several times and died.

Chapter 54

WHERE DO YOU suppose he lives?" he asked Clancy as he climbed out of the car and prompted her to jump out with him. She obliged.

"Well, not on this street," he said, as he saw nothing but empty lots.

Will walked randomly up the street and then down the next as he considered what to do. "I don't know that I'll recognize him. Even if we pass him." He frowned. "And we are not likely to find him by chance."

They returned to the car with the hope that it might start again. He held his breath and let out a huge sigh of relief when the engine turned over, once, twice … and … it started and sat there, purring like a cat, waiting for a saucer of milk.

He reversed the car and soon they were flying down a line of warehouses, and turning up the hill toward the next street.

Will drove down the next street, where he saw a cluster of houses, in a neat row, ahead of him. He hurried toward the houses.

FROM A DISTANCE, he watched the boy as he walked up the driveway of the house. Will liked the fact that it was not far from Edgewater Beach. He thought Clancy could be happy there. Not long afterward, he saw the boy and a man, who Will assumed was his father, playing catch in the front yard. Every little detail he noticed convinced him more that this was where Clancy belonged.

Will wasn't sure how long he would be able to hold Clancy off, once she saw the boy. And the fact that he was throwing a ball, complicated things further. So he walked back to the car with her and motioned for her to get in. He sat next to her, silently for a few minutes.

He took her head in between his hands, looked deep into her eyes and spoke softly. "Now, Clancy – it's very important for you to stay here and to be very quiet. It's time for all tired puppies to take a nap." He pulled out a biscuit from his jacket pocket and sat it next to her on the seat.

She tilted her head to one side, as if she actually understood. She lowered herself and rested her head on the seat.

"That's a good girl." He patted her gently on the head. "I will be back soon," he whispered.

Will returned to the house and walked up the steps to the front porch. He sat in the porch swing and he observed for a few minutes, with mixed emotions. And he reflected. It wasn't going to be easy for him, but he knew that he had to do what was best for Clancy.

He started down the steps to take another look around the yard, just to make sure that he didn't leave anything out of place - evidence that someone had been there.

As he walked through the garden, he felt like he was strolling through paradise. There were herbs, many of which he recognized, in beds that were separated by daisies. At the bottom of the garden was a slightly raised terrace where willowy lawn chairs, painted white, sat beneath a gazebo that was thick with wisteria vines, still green. That, he thought, was indicative of the boy's mother's nurturing spirit. – an excellent sign.

He nodded and disappeared around the side of the house and out onto the street. He could see Clancy moving around in the car as he approached and he was grateful that she hadn't been spotted.

Chapter 55

TWO DAYS LATER, the boy returned to Edgewater Beach, looking for the pooch he had seen. Hoping to keep the dog from running away from him again, he brought along something from home, thinking the pup might be hungry and hadn't eaten.

Will untied the rope from Clancy's collar and he tossed a small branch across the sand. And he watched. Clancy sprang into action sprinting across the beach, but she skidded to a sudden halt.

She lifted her nose in the air. The scent came to her. Filtered by the tangle of birds and rocks and squirrels crowding her, she recognized a scent that sent her sensitive nerves into a frenzy. She looked toward the cliff.

The moment Clancy spotted that ginger-colored hair, shining in the sunlight, she knew it was him. He was watching her.

As Clancy approached him, the boy slowly opened his hand and offered the hot dog to her. She never hesitated. She gobbled it up with the speed of a thousand gazelles.

What is this deliciousness?

The boy giggled with glee at the dog's reaction. What else could he do? He gave her the other two as well.

THAT NIGHT, WILL allowed Clancy to sleep up on the bed with him again, knowing that this could be their last night together. They nestled together as Will began to drift off into a peaceful sleep.

"Whew! **Clancy!** **What** *did you have to eat today?"*

THE *COMPASS ROSE* rocked gently, nudging him to wakefulness. Will woke up to bright sunshine and Clancy, staring at him, her muzzle planted on the edge of the bed, her brown eyes clear and bright.

He would not allow himself to think about how much he would miss her in the mornings. He was not going to let himself slide backward into that abyss of grief.

Chapter 56

SILHOUETTED IN PURPLE and gray shadows, the world was streaked with brilliant crimson colors of the sunset.

The boy, approaching the beach with his father, turned his eyes to observe a weathered rowboat, nearing the base of the cliffs. Nudging the dock with each wave, it lingered only for a few moments and then it turned back out onto the lake as the evening sun dissolved into the water.

He shaded his eyes and looked down the curve of the shore.

There was something near the pier -- *someone*. Metal clinked on metal as the shadow climbed onto the shore and shook, throwing water in all directions. The boy ran ahead and approached the rickety wooden dock.

She lifted her head at the crunch of shoes on the rocks above her, and then she turned and saw the boy heading her way.

The dog. "Hey Dad -- Look! It's the dog I told you about!"

Clancy's ears perked up at his voice and she broke into a slow trot, toward the boy. *It's him. The boy! There he is again.* The first thing she did was drop to the ground and roll over for a tummy rub. It was obvious. He was a she.

"Can I keep him, Dad? *Please?*"

The man tried, but he couldn't keep the smile from his face when he saw the spark in the seven-year-old's eyes. He and his wife had just made the decision that morning to find a dog for Dusty. "For starters, Dusty, I think *he* is a *she*."

"He looked up at his father. "She could be my birthday present ..." he pleaded with his dad, "... and *my Christmas present!*"

"Well, let's have a look, son." He knelt next to Dusty and the golden retriever and rubbed her neck, uncovering her collar.

Odd ...this looks more like a belt, cut to size, than a collar.

He looked at the attached metal tag. When he couldn't make out the weathered, timeworn etching that had once appeared on it, he flipped it to the opposite side. The man smiled. "It says her name is Clancy."

"*Clancy?*" Dusty grinned from ear to ear. "I like that name." He scruffed up her fur. "Hi Clancy." She slurped his face. Her tail wagged so hard that it looked like it would fly off.

Not far off the shoreline was a man sitting in a lifeboat, watching them intently through binoculars and thinly veiled tears of mixed emotions. Will knew he ought to be glad that Clancy would be acclimated. That her eyes were on the boy and off of him. He wanted her to be happy. He wanted to be happy for her and he would be. Eventually.

He blinked heavily twice, comprehending the magnitude of what was happening. Then he sighed, and a small smile eased across his face. While it was a smile of happiness and relief, it was certainly not the smile of victory.

"She might be lost," Dusty's father told him. He grinned down at his son, who was in an obvious state of euphoria. "Tell you what - we'll take her home for now. I'll post signs saying we found her. But if her owners call us, you know we'll have to give her back to them, don't you?" the boy's father said.

But Dusty didn't hear him. He was too busy fussing over Clancy. It was a forever moment - a moment that would make anyone's heart bigger.

"Come on, girl -- let's go home."

Chapter 57

WILLIAM STOCKTON DROPPED his cigarette at the sight - the captain of the schooner, standing there in the darkness, his eyes shining and filled with triumph.

Will quickly regained his composure. Somehow, just the captain's presence with him, on the deck of the *Compass Rose*, gave him the sense, at least for the moment, that he could handle whatever it was he would have to face.

The captain's eyes narrowed as he leaned forward. *"Ah, you remember me?"*

Will met his eyes. "Why shouldn't I remember you? You're the one who is responsible for all of this."

He threw back his head and laughed. *"Guilty as charged. But only as far as choosing you to carry on what we started. You were already caught in the loop when we met."*

"The dog ..." the captain asked him - or perhaps Will only thought he asked. *"... Safe?"*

Will grinned. "Yes."

The captain smiled and nodded to Will.

"We did it," Will said. "You and me and the *Compass Rose*. Clancy and the legend are safe."

"Clancy ... Ruddy Warrior ... Good..."

Profound relief passed through Will.

The captain said, *"You seem to have taken great strides since I last saw you."* He was becoming increasingly more transparent as he retreated.

Will started to speak to him again. "Captain ..." but he raised a hand and spoke again. *"Regret for what has been - or for what might have been is ... folly - a waste of precious time and energy. Do not give your future to the past. Do not look back."* A ghost of a smile flitted across his face, lightening the mood.

Will tried again. "Captain - You wrote, in the log that we must reach down into ourselves for courage and strength. But I think we reached out to each other."

"I do not doubt that important things are going to happen to you. The Compass Rose is a very extraordinary vessel. Know that wherever you're going, you are never alone."

His voice was intense and his expression glowing. *"Remember, we feel what you feel."* His image completely faded into thin air.

Will searched through the darkness for him, in the beginning stages of panic. "Wait!" He sat down hard in the chair, in frustration. But he was answered with a whisper, delivered by the Lake Erie breeze.

"The oceans never stop, my friend. Nor do the lakes. They know no beginning or end. The wind never ceases. Sometimes it will disappear, but only to gather momentum from elsewhere, returning to cast itself back in your presence."

The voice returned for one more, much more emphatic message.

"Keep your eyes - and your heart - open. This is not the end."

Chapter 58

NOTHING IN LIFE is certain, and there are no guarantees.

The lives they knew were gone forever. But in their place, they had been given another chance - the opportunity to make a difference.

Overhead, the birds were suspiciously silent as a great hush settled over *the Compass Rose*.

Yeager's voice broke the silence. "I've got the captain, Will. He looks a might under the weather again, I'm afraid."

Will exhaled and tossed his cigarette butt over the rail. He sighed. "Tell the wheelsman that I will remain here. I'll sit with him in the pilot house again tonight." He turned and faced the darkness of the vast sea before him. "Don't be so hard on Hale. I suppose some habits are hard to break …"

He swallowed his words and dropped his jaw as he watched his incomplete sentence separate, floating up into the night and coming to rest there, glittering in bright points.

Maybe this is how the stars were conceived - each one the finale of a fragmented thought.

William Stockton allowed himself a slight grin, wishing that his brother John could have seen him during the past months. Perhaps somewhere, somehow, John would realize that Will didn't need him to make wise decisions.

Things were different now. Now it wasn't about practicalities, risk assessment, or smart decision-making. Nor was it about the schooner. It was about the *Compass Rose.*

As his thoughts went on, more fear began to dissipate, replaced by a warm infusion of something else. Peace. Assurance. Confidence. Not in himself, in his abilities, but in the legend that had brought him to this place in time.

Over the lake, lightning flashed - a classic thunderbolt straight from the gods. Another tempest was brewing, and they both could feel it. Thunder rolled, closer now. Will looked out at the swirling, tempestuous water. He suddenly realized with the force of the next lightning bolt that they were heading straight into the whirlwind.

He beamed at the dark clouds as if he were greeting old friends and buttoned his jacket up to his throat against the gale winds. The *Compass Rose* began to creak under the burden of the impending storm.

Yeager hoisted Captain Hale over his shoulder and followed Will into the pilothouse. In a voice just above a murmur, he asked,

"Where will we go from here?"

Will sensed the question was more spiritual than geographical. He felt another sense of calmness settle over him. He leaned forward, placed the captain's hat on his head and he took another swipe at the orange-encrusted housefly droning around his ear. He positioned his hands firmly on the wheel.

Will faced the helm and he smiled.

"I have no idea."

The "Great Miami" Hurricane was first spotted as a tropical wave located 1,000 miles east of the Lesser Antilles on September 11, 1926. The system moved quickly westward and intensified to hurricane strength as it moved to the north of Puerto Rico on the 15th. Winds were reported to be nearly 150 mph as the hurricane passed over the Turks Islands on the 16th and through the Bahamas on the 17th.

Credit: National Hurricane Center and Central Pacific Hurricane Center

---

Amelia Earhart, born on July 24, 1897 in Atchison, Kansas, was the first woman to fly solo across the Atlantic Ocean.

In her passion for flying, she accumulated a number of distance and altitude world records. But beyond her accomplishments as a pilot, she also sought to make a statement about the role and worth of women. She dedicated much of her life to prove that women could excel in their chosen professions just like men and have equal value. This contributed to her wide appeal and international celebrity.

Amelia's unsolved disappearance during a flight around the world in 1937 became an enduring mystery, fueling much speculation and giving her lasting recognition in popular culture as one of the world's most celebrated aviators.

Credit: Biography.com
Credit: Encyclopedia Britannica